THE INVITATION

ERIKA WILDE

Welcome to the players club!
Erika Wilde

Copyright © Erika Wilde, January 2014

All rights reserved. No part of this book may be used or reproduced in any manner whatsoever without permission except in the case of brief quotations embodied in critical articles and reviews. This book is a work of fiction. Names, characters, places and incidents are either products of the author's imagination or used fictitiously. Any resemblance to actual events, locals, or persons, living or dead, is entirely coincidental. All rights reserved. No part of this publication can be reproduced or transmitted in any form or by any means, electronic or mechanical, without permission in writing from the Author.

CHAPTER 1

"I can't believe you're getting a drink with me instead of going home to your wife. Don't *even* tell me that there's trouble in paradise."

Dean grinned at his best friend, Brent "Mac" MacMillan, who sat on a bar stool beside him at a local joint they frequented after work to relax and unwind. Though, admittedly, ever since Jillian had shown up at Dean's office weeks ago and propositioned him with spicing up their sex lives, he'd spent a helluva lot more time at home with his wife, than hanging out with the guys.

"Trust me, the only reason I'm sitting

here with you instead of being at home with Jillian is because I have a huge favor to ask."

"Anything," Mac said sincerely. "Just ask and it's yours."

Dean knew he spoke the truth because they'd always had each other's backs. They'd met in the Navy and served in the same SEAL platoon and were now business partners at Noble and Associates, the security firm that Dean and Mac had established when they'd retired from the military a few years ago. The two of them had started the company doing oddball security gigs, but with their training and experience they'd quickly become a prominent, multi-million dollar firm specializing in executive protection and corporate threat management.

Becoming a successful, viable corporation had taken a lot of time and dedication on both their parts, but all the blood, sweat, and leaner times had been well worth the sacrifice. Dean couldn't imagine any other partner than Mac. He was the brother Dean never had, and the one person he trusted implicitly.

Dean took a drink from his bottle of beer before getting to the point of the conversation. "Remember a few years ago when you asked if I was interested in an invitation to The Players Club?" The Players Club, a huge, massive estate located outside of San Diego in the hills of Fallbrook, was an exclusive, members-only society that catered to the erotic and forbidden. The only way to get inside the private, elite mansion was by invitation only by a current member, which Mac was.

"Yeah, I remember," Mac replied, a hint of curiosity tingeing his drawl. "And I distinctly recall you turning down the offer saying it wasn't Jillian's thing. Has that changed?"

"Possibly." He'd never brought up the subject of The Players Club to his wife, but considering how open-minded Jillian had become, he figured it was a good time to introduce yet another fantasy he'd entertained for years. And with their twentieth anniversary coming up, it seemed like the perfect gift, for the both of them.

Mac studied Dean for a moment before realization dawned. "Does this have anything to do with that day when Jillian dropped by your office, the two of you spent some time alone, and she left with a big smile on her face and looking a bit disheveled?"

"Noticed that, did you?"

A knowing smirk curved the corner of Mac's lips. "Along with the fact that you couldn't concentrate on shit after she walked out."

Dean laughed, unable to deny his friend's claim. He had very fond memories of that day in his office—the day that changed so much between him and his wife, for the better. "Jillian has decided that with both the boys grown and out of the house, it's time to focus on us and making our sex life more interesting and daring."

"And how's that working out?" Mac asked before finishing off his beer.

"Fucking fantastic." Dean grinned. He wasn't one to share details, but he had to admit that even beyond the phenomenal sex, they'd become closer as a couple. Their relationship was more intimate, their interaction on a daily basis more fun and flirty.

"Lucky bastard," Mac muttered begrudgingly.

"What are you complaining about?" Dean asked, amused by his friend's envious statement. "You always have some hot bombshell ready and willing to warm your bed."

"Not the same thing." Mac sighed as he absently wiped away the condensation on his beer bottle with his fingers. "You're lucky because your marriage has lasted nearly twenty years and you still seem to be enjoying a smokin' hot sex life. Do you know how rare that is?"

Realizing which road they were suddenly traveling, Dean grew serious. "You tried really hard to make your marriage work, Mac. You just rescued the wrong woman, and you never should have married her."

Mac's lips thinned, as they always did whenever they talked about the one woman who'd ripped his heart out and stomped on it for good measure. "I'm done rescuing. Period. It's not worth the fucking hassle or emotional turmoil."

Dean didn't argue, and just hoped that the *right* woman came along to change Mac's mind someday. But at the age of thirty-six, Mac was set in his ways and certain he was better off a bachelor who kept things simple and temporary. And being a member of The Players Club offered him easy, uncomplicated sex with a woman who enjoyed the same level of kink that he did.

"So, do you think Jillian is ready for a place like The Players Club?" Mac asked, effectively changing the subject off him and his failed marriage.

"I think she could be, yes," Dean replied. "She's become more adventurous lately, so I'd like to give her the option of accepting the invitation, or not, though I'm *not* interested in swinging or sharing." As he'd already learned that night she'd taken him to a night club, that point was absolutely non-negotiable.

"Trust me, there's something for everyone at The Players Club," Mac said, obviously speaking from his own personal experience. "And there are certain basic rules, and everyone abides by them or they're immediately banned. Nobody's going to touch Jillian."

"Not if they value their lives," Dean said, meaning it.

Mac chuckled and pushed his empty beer bottle across the bar. "Are you sure she'll be okay?" he asked, concern lacing his voice. "And I'm not referring to just the sexual atmosphere, but the fact that she'll know people there. Like me, and a lot of our other guys."

Dean had already thought about that. "You've already assured me that there is a confidentiality clause in the contract that everyone signs, so I'm assuming that whatever happens at the club, stays at the club?"

Mac nodded. "Yes, and for those clients who don't know you, there are no last names exchanged to protect your privacy, as well."

Which was all very reassuring to Dean.

"Then it's up to Jillian and how comfortable she is with everything." She would be the deciding factor, because he wasn't going to put his wife in situation that made her uneasy.

"Fair enough," Mac said in understanding. "I'll make a call and you should have the invitation in a few days."

"Perfect." Just in time for their twentieth anniversary. "I appreciate it."

JILLIAN WALKED into Sugar and Spice, an upscale adult boutique that specialized in selling fun, sexy toys, gorgeous lingerie, and other erotic novelty items. Located in a cluster of other specialty type businesses that catered to a sophisticated clientele, Sugar and Spice had become one of her favorite places to shop lately, and had provided her and Dean with plenty of sensual ideas to help fulfill many of their fantasies.

Ultimately, this store had helped to revive her marriage, had increased her confidence as a woman, and had given her husband the permission to truly embrace that dominant alpha male in the bedroom. Or rather, their newly designed playroom, which was now filled with all sorts of provocative toys and gadgets.

"Hey, Jillian," a familiar female voice greeted her.

"Hi, Raina," Jillian returned, smiling at the beautiful blonde haired woman who owned the boutique, and who had also become a good friend.

It was early afternoon, and the store was quiet. Other than Aaron—a good looking, muscular guy who doubled as a bodyguard for Raina, and as a sales person when needed—there wasn't anyone else in the place. From across the store in the video section, Aaron acknowledged her with a friendly nod before returning to stocking the shelves.

Raina came around the front counter, wearing a pair of white denim jeans, a pink top, and a pair of high heels that accentuated her long legs. The woman had a body of a centerfold, and Jillian had seen many male customers stare at her with obvious lust, but she never returned their interest or flirtatious, persuasive come-ons. Raina had once told Jillian that she never mixed business with pleasure, and considering she owned an adult boutique, dating men always came with certain expectations she had no intentions of fulfilling.

"What brings you in today?" Raina asked, always eager to help.

"I'm looking for some sexy lingerie to wear," Jillian said.

"I thought I heard Jillian's voice!" Another woman appeared from the back of the store carrying a few hangers displaying her gorgeous, one-of-a-kind corset creations that she sold at Sugar and Spice, and commissioned for customers. "A lady can never have enough sexy lingerie, that's for sure."

Jillian grinned at Paige, a red-head with voluptuous curves who wasn't afraid to flaunt them, and an outrageous personality that always amused Jillian. "So true."

Raina looped her arm through Jillian's and guided her toward the lingerie section.

"Did you have something particular in mind?"

"Maybe another corset?" Paige piped in, lifting one of the satin-lined hangers to reveal a stunning bustier made with emerald satin, pearls, and feathers. "I just finished this one this morning, and I have to admit I'm having a hard time putting it on display, instead of keeping it for myself."

Jillian could understand why. The corset was exotic and seductive, yet fun, too. "My husband loved the red leather corset you custom made for me," she said, thinking back to when she'd played the dominatrix to her husband's slave in the playroom a few weeks ago. "But I think I want something more elegant."

Raina raised a curious brow. "Special occasion coming up?"

"Yes, my twentieth anniversary," she said as she looked through a rack of baby doll nighties—all pretty and sexy, but nothing that wowed her.

Paige's green eyes rounded in shock. "Oh my God, did Dean rob the cradle with you?"

"You don't look old enough to be married twenty years!" Raina added, equally stunned.

Jillian laughed. "Thanks for the compliment, but I'm thirty-eight."

Paige arranged one of her corsets on a display mannequin. "So, you were eighteen when you got married?" she asked, obviously having done the quick math in her head. "And you're *still* married?"

"Yes, and yes," Jillian said in answer to each question. "Happily so."

"And clearly, Dean is still crazy about you," Raina said, a soft, wistful sigh escaping her. "Whenever he comes in here and mentions your name, he always gets this crazy-sexy grin on his face."

Yes, she was very fortunate to have a husband who still adored her.

"What do you think of this?" Raina asked, holding up a sheer red chemise trimmed in black lace for her to see.

"Too short and revealing," Jillian said with a shake of her head, knowing if Dean saw that on her he'd be way too distracted. She wanted to tease him, not turn him into the uncontrollable sexy beast he became whenever he saw her naked. That outfit would be like waving a red flag in front of a perpetual horny bull, she thought in amusement. "I'd like something sexy, yet subtle and romantic," she told Raina.

"Gotcha. You want to leave a little to the imagination."

Jillian grinned. "Exactly."

Raina nodded in understanding and headed toward a rack displaying more luxurious, high end lingerie. "So, what made you get married so young?" she asked curiously as she looked through the selection of rich silks, clearly looking for something specific.

"I got knocked up," Jillian replied.

A startled look transformed Raina's expression, and embarrassment pinkened her cheeks. "Oh, God, I'm so sorry . . . I didn't mean to be nosey . . . it really isn't any of my business."

Jillian chuckled at Raina's flustered composure. "It's not a big deal. I was young, in love, and it was hard to resist Dean's bad boy charm," she said honestly, though it had been more than just his tough, sexy image and cajoling ways that had led her to give Dean her virginity at the age of seventeen.

She could clearly recall that fateful night, when she'd seen such agony in his eyes and discovered just how wounded he was on the inside, that beneath his rough, I'm-a-rebel personality was a boy who was scarred by a father's verbal and physical abuse. And despite being a good girl who always followed her parent's strict rules, she'd ignored their disapproval of Dean and followed her heart.

That dark, stormy night, his pain had become her own and all she'd wanted was to let him know that he was loved, so she'd replaced his torment with the deepest, most intimate thing she could give him. Her body and innocence.

Getting pregnant certainly hadn't been part of the plan, but twenty years later she could look back and know that it all happened the way it was supposed to. Dean was her soul-mate and there wasn't anything up to this point that she'd change about her life.

But now that the kids were grown and gone, a part of her was starting to feel restless and sometimes even bored—not with her marriage, but her daily routine. There was nothing to fill her time while Dean was at work, nothing that gave her a reason to wake up excited in the morning or left her with a sense of accomplishment at the end of the day. Her entire world had revolved around her husband and boys for nearly twenty years, and now that she had too much time on her hands she was beginning to crave something for *herself.*

Even if she did have an idea in mind, she wasn't sure how Dean would react to her taking a job when he was a man who'd made it very clear that he would take care of his wife and family—in all the ways his father never had. Dean had always been determined that she'd never have to work and prided himself on being the sole provider. For her, it wasn't about the money, but she wasn't sure that he could differentiate the two in his mind, considering the emotionally painful dynamics between his own mother and father.

Jillian shook those thoughts from her head, and redirected her mind to the conversation at hand between herself, Raina, and Paige. "I know getting pregnant wasn't an ideal situation for a teenager in high school," Jillian admitted. "But I have two great boys and a husband who is-"

"Hotter and more sinful than the devil himself," Paige interrupted with her own interpretation of Dean.

"Paige!" Raina said, scolding her friend for her candid outburst.

"What, it's the truth," Paige replied unapologetically, her hands on her curvy hips. "That man is sex on a stick and there is nothing wrong with me visually appreciating that fine body of his. Isn't that right, Jillian?"

Jillian couldn't argue with Paige's logic. "Hey, the 'you can look but don't touch' rule certainly works for me." Actually, she found Paige's description of Dean flattering. It was nice to know that other women were envious, and Jillian was secure enough in her relationship and marriage to feel no threat whatsoever.

"Ah, here it is," Raina announced as she pulled a hanger from the rack. "I think this is *exactly* what you're looking for. Subtly sexy, but soft and romantic."

Jillian took one look at the negligee and knew it was the one. "I'd love to try it on."

A few minutes later she was in the dressing room, her heart rate speeding up in excitement as she stared at her reflection in the three way mirror. The long gown was made of cool black silk that draped seductively across her body and hinted at her curves. Thin straps gave way to a loose bodice that caressed her breasts, rather than molding to them. The right side had a thigh-high slit to show a flash of bare leg when she walked, or sat down, and where that ended ribbons laced up the rest of the negligee, adding a little temptation to the otherwise demure gown and giving the illusion that with one little tug of the bow it would all unravel and fall away.

When she walked out of the room, Raina was waiting nearby for her.

"Well?" her friend asked expectantly. "What did you think?"

"It's perfect. I'll take it."

"And look what else I found." Grinning, Raina held up a pair of men's black silk pajama pants for Dean.

While Dean preferred wearing his old, worn cotton sweat pants around the house, Jillian loved the idea of them wearing a matching set for their anniversary and adding a little sensual luxury to the special night. "I'll take those, too." Jillian handed Raina the negligee and followed the other woman up to the front counter.

"So, do you have big plans for your milestone anniversary?" Raina asked as she clipped the tags from the gown and wrapped up Jillian's purchases in pretty pink tissue paper.

"Just a nice, quiet, romantic dinner for two at home." It's what Jillian wanted, even though Dean had given her the choice to go out to a fancy restaurant. She had the entire meal planned and was looking forward to a more intimate setting with her husband, just the two of them.

"Sounds lovely." Raina rang up the transaction and swiped Jillian's credit card.

"And I'm sure he's going to love the gift you had done for him."

"I think so, too. I can't wait to give it to him." Her gift wasn't a traditional anniversary present, but there was no doubt in her mind that Dean was going to thoroughly enjoy the surprise—and she had Raina to thank for the fantastic idea. "Thanks again for the recommendation."

"I'm happy to help," Raina said, waving away her gratitude. "And it helps my friends, too. Kendall told me that the pictures turned out *amazing*."

"Oh, they did," Jillian assured her with a smile.

"Here you go." Raina handed her a pink Sugar and Spice bag with her new lingerie and Dean's silk pajama pants. "I hope you have a wonderful anniversary. Dean is one lucky man."

Jillian truly believed that *she* was the fortune one, in so many ways. "Well, there's no doubt in my mind that he's going to *get* lucky," she said, and left the shop with Raina's laughter trailing behind her.

CHAPTER 2

Dean walked into the house, his stomach growling hungrily as he was greeted by the delicious aroma of the pork roast Jillian had been slow-cooking all afternoon for their anniversary dinner. He'd spent the past three hours with his guys at a martial arts studio, running through training and conditioning exercises, which everyone was required to attend the first Saturday of the month. Dean's muscles were sore, in a good way, and all that aggression had given him a nice adrenaline rush he was still feeling.

He found Jillian in the kitchen, wearing her red silk robe and her hair gathered and clipped atop her head as she reached for the good china plates in the cupboard. The short hem of her robe inched up as she stood on her tiptoes and stretched her arm toward the third shelf, giving him a glimpse of pretty white lace panties and the sweet curve of her ass.

She was so intent on her task that she hadn't heard him walk in, and when he came up behind her and easily grabbed the plates for her, she gasped in startled surprise.

She spun around, her hand on her heart. "Dammit, Dean, you know I hate it when you sneak up on me!" she scolded.

He chuckled and braced his hands on either side of her on the counter. "I wasn't trying to be quiet."

"No, you just *are*," she said, her lips pursed in exasperation. "Stealth mode is your normal method of operation."

A trait ingrained from his SEAL days. "Maybe you ought to hang a bell around my neck so you can hear me coming."

The corner of her mouth twitched with a smile. "Don't tempt me."

Seeing his favorite meal on the stovetop, he inhaled deeply and his stomach rumbled again. "Dinner smells amazing."

Her gaze took in his disheveled hair, the stubble on his jaw, and his sweat stained muscle shirt he'd worn for his work-out. She wrinkled her nose at him. "Everything is just about ready. Go and take a shower, and I'll leave you something to wear on the bed."

"You mean we aren't going to have a naked anniversary dinner?" He tugged on the sash around her waist, loosening the tie. "Could be fun."

She rolled her eyes and lightly smacked his hand away. "If we were naked, we'd never get around to eating."

"Oh, *I* certainly would," he said, waggling his brows meaningfully.

The flare of heat in her eyes completely contradicted the stern look she managed to give him. "Go shower *now*, Dean, or you're not eating at all." She pointed toward the hallway.

"Spoil sport," he teased, and dropped a

quick kiss on her lips before heading toward their bedroom.

He peeled off his damp clothes and stepped beneath the hot shower spray. He soaped up, rinsed off, and took the time to give himself a close shave so he didn't leave burn marks on Jillian's soft skin. It was their anniversary, after all, and he decided that he'd give his wife a night of romance—hearts and flowers and all that shit that women liked every so often—instead of rough and wild sex.

Done showering, he dried off, then tucked the towel around his hips as he brushed his teeth and blow-dried his hair so that it wasn't dripping wet. He rubbed her favorite after shave along his now smooth jaw, before tossing the towel into the hamper and strolling back into the bedroom bare-ass naked. Just as she promised, she'd laid out something for him to wear.

He frowned as he picked up the black silk lounging pants, which were so not his thing and a little too metro-sexual for his taste. But considering Jillian had bought them for him, he put them on and tightened the drawstring around his waist, unsure how he felt about the slip and slide texture of the material in masculine places.

Geez, the things he wouldn't do for his wife, he thought with a shake of his head.

There was no shirt, so he assumed she wanted his chest bare, which was more than fine with him. Before heading back to Jillian, he stopped in his office and retrieved the white square envelope he'd hidden away in one of the desk drawers beneath some files. The word "welcome" was embossed in black on the front of the envelope, giving no real hint as to what was tucked inside.

As he headed back down the hallway, he realized that the lights in the kitchen were now off, and a soft glow of light from the formal dining area beckoned to him. He stepped into the room that they only used for holidays or special occasions, and was taken aback by the transformation that greeted him.

She'd taken a few dwarf trees and wrapped twinkling lights around them, giving the room an enchanting, fairy-tale like glow. Half a dozen candles flickered around the bouquet of twenty long-stemmed roses on the table he'd had delivered to her earlier in the day, and she'd already served up their dinner, using her best china, silver, and crystal.

He shifted his gaze to his wife, who was standing nearby. As corny as it even sounded to him, his heart skipped a beat at the realization that this sweet, beautiful woman was all his. In the twenty minutes that he'd been gone, she'd managed to transform herself into what he could only describe as a sensual, gorgeous goddess.

She'd taken the clip from atop her head, allowing all that soft, glorious hair to fall around her bare shoulders, her skin glowing from the warmth of the candlelight. The material of her black silk negligee matched his pajama pants, and the cut of the gown hinted at her luscious curves, rather than boldly enhancing them. The thin fabric skimmed across her full breasts, highlighting the tight peak of her nipples. His gaze fell to the tempting slit exposing her right leg, all the way up to her hip, where silk laces criss-crossed and secured the side of the gown. Her bare skin showed through, making him well aware of the fact that she wasn't wearing any panties beneath.

His dick appreciated that fact a whole lot. Desire licked through him, settling in his groin, and as much as he wanted to skip dinner and feast on Jillian instead, he reined in his randy body so he didn't ruin whatever she had planned.

"Happy Anniversary, darling," she said, strolling toward him, a sensual smile on her lips.

"Yes, *very* happy," he agreed. He propped the envelope against the glass vase for her to open later, right next to a wrapped present with his name on it, then pulled her into his embrace and lowered his mouth to hers.

Their lips met, and she wrapped her arms around his neck and sighed as he deepened the kiss. His tongue swept in and tangled with hers, slow and thorough, a seductive, delightful preview to how he intended to end this evening. Before lust could completely fog his brain, he eased back and glanced down into her upturned face. Her still parted lips were damp and puffy, and that unconditional, adoring look in her hazy eyes made him feel like the luckiest man alive.

"Let's eat before it gets cold," he said, releasing her.

"Good idea," she said, amusement in her tone. "The sooner we finish dinner, the better."

He couldn't agree more, but knowing how much time and care she'd taken in making this anniversary meal special, he didn't want to rush.

He sat at the head of the table like he always did, and she took the seat beside him. He reached for the bottle of champagne chilling in a bucket of ice, released the cork, and poured them each a glass of the Cristal. They picked up their crystal flutes and toasted to the occasion.

"To the best twenty years of my life," Jillian said, and took a drink of the sparkling wine. "We've come a long ways, wouldn't you say?"

He set his glass back on the table and grinned wryly. "Yeah, we've made it twenty years longer than what your parents ever thought we'd last."

She picked up her fork and knife and carved into the slice of pork roast on her plate. "When it came to you, I never put much stock in what my parents thought, or believed, or expected. I never, ever, doubted that you'd take care of me and our babies."

And it had been that unwavering trust and faith in him that had turned Dean from a brash, reckless teenager who'd been heading down a path of personal destruction, and into a man determined to take care of the one thing that mattered to him in a world that had been so bleak and dark before she'd been assigned to tutor him in calculus his senior year in high school.

Those after school lessons had changed everything. He'd been angry and bitter, and hating the fact that one of the most popular and prettiest girls in school had to help him wrap his brain around derivatives and algebraic notations. Yet despite his surly attitude that first day, she'd been patient and kind and not at all intimidated by his bad boy reputation.

Meeting with her after school soon became the highlight of his day and gave him something to look forward to, even if he'd spent more time thinking about kissing her soft lips than mathematical equations. And it hadn't taken long for him to realize that she kept looking at his mouth, too. After a few weeks of denying their strong attraction, he'd given into the urge to taste her lips, and thought he'd died and gone to heaven when she returned his kiss.

Jillian had been a good girl, a straight A student and the daughter of a prominent family who'd already funded the way for her to attend a private college, and who didn't approve of a boy from the wrong side of town with no future goals in mind. Dean had known that he was all wrong for her, that he never should have touched her, but he'd been so drawn to her sweet innocence, her genuine smiles, her interest in *him* as a person, that he'd been unable to resist her.

She made him *laugh* when he'd forgotten how. She made him *want* when he'd stopped believing in anything good. She'd pulled him out of a grim existence and had given him something to hope for. She'd made him *feel* when he'd thought his father's physical and verbal abuse had stripped him of the ability to care for anyone or anything.

Jillian getting pregnant had been completely unplanned, but it had been a gift in disguise that had transformed him from a boy with no direction, into a man committed to give her everything she needed and deserved. Going against her parent's demands that they give the baby up for adoption, he'd instead married Jillian as soon as she turned eighteen, then joined the Navy for a steady paycheck that would support her and their baby, and eventually trained to join the Navy SEALs.

Every penny he'd earned was sent to Jillian, to pay the rent on their tiny studio apartment, and to take care of her and their sons, who'd been born less than fifteen months apart. Those first few years being separated had been extremely hard and difficult, but he'd been determined that she'd never have to work, a decision that tied directly to his own mother, who'd worked two jobs to support the family because his father was a drunk who couldn't hold down any job for any length of time.

The horrible memories of his tired, exhausted mother getting home late at night, only to be greeted by a beating because she couldn't make dinner fast enough for Dean's father, was something he'd never be able to forget. The terrible cycle repeated itself daily, until his mother just gave up and overdosed on sleeping pills to escape the physical and emotional pain, leaving Dean with a wealth of guilt for not being able to save her from such a cruel and dreadful life.

"Hey, where did you go?" Jillian asked softly, pulling him back to the present. "And what are you frowning about?"

He shrugged, pushed those unpleasant thoughts from his mind, and smiled at her as he swallowed a bite of his buttered green beans. "I was just thinking about all those lean years we had in the beginning of our marriage." And not once had she complained, or left him for someone better as he always feared she would. She'd always supported him and his goals, no matter that it meant months of separation while he worked his way up the military ladder, so to speak.

"It was definitely a tough time," she agreed, cutting into an herbed potato. "But look at you now. You're a successful businessman, making more money than my father does," she said, and laughed.

"Look at *us* now," he clarified, knowing she was the reason for everything he had. Jillian's faith in him slayed him. She was his salvation, his reason for turning his life around when he'd been so close to not giving a shit about anything and probably would have turned out just like his old man if it hadn't been for her giving him something to truly live for.

"I like where we are," she said happily, unaware of his darker thoughts as she sipped the last bit of her champagne. "And I really like where we're heading. You've spent so many years working hard and making sacrifices so you could give me all *this*—" she waved a hand to indicate the custom built home, the furnishings, the comfortable life she lived, "—and now it's your turn to enjoy it, too."

"*You* deserve all this, and more," he said, meaning it.

"I have everything I want right here with you. All this other *stuff* is just a nice extra bonus."

They were both finished with their dinner, and he pushed his plate aside then scooted out his chair. "Come here," he said, wanting her close. "I want to give you your anniversary gift."

She stood up then settled herself on his lap, fitting so perfectly against him. Resting one hand around her waist, he reached for the envelope he'd left on the table and handed it to her.

She took it from him and ran her

fingers over the one word printed on the front of the heavy linen envelope. "Welcome?" she asked curiously as she met his gaze. "It looks like an invitation of some sort."

He shrugged off the sudden jolt of nervousness spreading through him. "Open it and you'll see."

She slid her finger beneath the flap and pulled out the card tucked inside. "You are cordially invited to The Players Club," she said, her voice trailing off as she silently read the rest of the invitation. When she was done, she lifted her wide-eyed gaze to his. "The Players Club?" she asked, her tone hesitant.

That uncertainty swirling in his gut escalated a notch. "Yes," he said calmly, worried that he was pushing her way outside of her comfort zone. "Do you know what that is?"

A slight frown marred her expression, giving him no real clue as to what she was truly thinking. "Yes, I've heard of it before. It's a sex club, right?"

He nodded and stroked a hand along

her back in a gentle caress. "A very exclusive, private, members-only club. I just thought we might enjoy trying something new and different."

She glanced down at the card in her hand again, studying it for a moment before meeting his gaze. "If it's so private, how did you get this invitation?"

"Mac." He grinned.

She raised an incredulous brow. "He's a member?"

"A lot of the guys that work for me are," he told her, wanting to make sure she realized that fact ahead of time. "In order to get an invitation into The Players Club, you need a referral from a long-term member in good standing. The club also requires every person to pass a confidential background check and health screening before their first visit, which we'll have done if you agree you'd like to do this." As a security specialist, Dean liked the fact that every individual had to pass a thorough application process and that there were discreet guidelines to follow. The exorbitant membership fee also helped to ensure exclusivity.

"Do *you* want this?" she asked.

"Yes, but what I want doesn't matter. It's your choice, not mine." It was important to him that she desired the same thing, and wasn't agreeing just to please him. They'd come a long ways since that day she'd seduced him in his office, but the possibility did exist that she wasn't ready to take such a huge leap to a sex club. "I don't want you to feel pressured in any way if you're not okay with any of this."

Biting her bottom lip, she worried the soft piece of flesh between her teeth before asking what seemingly concerned her the most. "Do they swap couples there?"

The insecurity touching her features felt like a fist to his chest, and he sought to reassure her. "It's definitely an option for members, but not a requirement, and there are public and private rooms, depending on a couple's preference. I've been assured that monogamy is respected and I have no intention of sharing you with *anyone*," he said adamantly. "Have you already forgotten how crazy jealous and possessive it made me to see another man put his hands on you at the night club?"

She ducked her head and laughed, though he didn't miss the adorable blush on her cheeks. "I remember everything, especially *afterwards*."

He let out a low, playful growl, recalling how much she'd loved his primal, alpha, *your-my-woman* claiming of her once they'd gotten home. "Yeah, that part was fun."

Setting the invitation on the table, she turned more fully towards him on his lap and placed her cool palms on either side of his face, holding his gaze with her very somber one. "Just to be very clear, I don't want to share you with anyone, either. They can look all they want, but no touching, unless you'd like to see a cat fight break out between two grown women, complete with nail scratching and hair pulling."

"That sounds totally hot." He smirked.

She playfully smacked his bare chest. "I'm serious," she said, though she was smiling. "Looking is allowed, but absolutely no touching."

He gave her a very solemn look. "Agreed."

She exhaled a soft breath. "Then yes, I want to go to The Players Club with you."

He blinked at her, surprised by her quick decision. "Are you sure?"

"Absolutely, positively sure." She gave him an adorably sheepish look. "Truthfully, I've always wondered what it would be like to go to a sex club, so I can at least scratch that off my to-do list."

"Or add it to our must-do-again list," he suggested, just for the hell of it.

"We'll see," she said, not committing beyond that initial visit, which he completely understood.

She reached across the table and grabbed the wrapped gift with his name on it. "I hope you like *your* anniversary present."

Now *she* looked nervous, which made him curious to know what she'd bought for him. He took the present from her, and while she watched anxiously, he tore away the paper and revealed a leather bound photo book. The cover was engraved in gold lettering with *To Dean, the love of my life. Happy Twentieth Anniversary.*

She shifted on his lap, and he opened the cover to the first page, expecting to see photographs chronicling their twenty years together, but instead his jaw nearly dropped to his chest when he laid eyes on the first full-sized, glossy picture of Jillian in glorious color detail.

This wasn't an ordinary snapshot, either. No, this image of her, dressed in a sexy, all white baby doll nightie made his heart hammer excitedly in his chest, and his dick pulse with desire. She was kneeling on the bed in their playroom, staring at the camera with a provocative come-hither look in her slumberous eyes and a tempting smile on her beautiful face. Her hands were propped on her bare knees, which were slightly spread, and the way she leaned forward pushed her full breasts up and out. Through the sheer lace, he could see her dark pink areolas, and her hard nipples.

"Holy shit, Jill," he breathed, both shocked and incredibly turned on by the unexpected photograph. "Who the hell took this photo?" If it was a guy, he'd have to hunt him down and kill him, he thought, only half-joking.

"A friend of Raina's. Her name is Kendall and she's a photographer who also does private boudoir sessions for clients. Do you like it?"

He gave her a wry look. "Can you honestly not feel how hard my dick is against your ass?" he said, and laughed.

She wriggled on his lap, rubbing herself against his stiff cock, and he groaned. "Ahh, yes, that's very telling," she teased, nuzzling her lips along his neck. "Turn the page. There's plenty more for you to see."

He did as she requested and again was blown away by the hot, playboyish type shots that had been captured of his wife in different poses and stages of dress—and undress. Each picture was tasteful, yet undeniably erotic. The woman who'd taken each photograph had played up Jillian's best assets—her voluptuous breasts, her ass, and that soft curve of her hips. All the features that drove him mad with lust, and even now he could feel that hunger for her pounding through his veins as he gazed at a print of Jillian laying on her side in a red lace bra and matching panties, garter belt, and stockings. The sultry look in her eyes said *I'm yours. Come and get me.*

"Just so you know, you were the inspiration for every look and pose you see," she whispered as her soft mouth moved along his jawline and her fingers plucked at his rigid nipples. "I glanced into that camera like it was *you* looking at me, wanting me, and it made me feel so hot and sexy."

He exhaled a harsh breath that did nothing to ease the sexual tension building within him, though he was pretty sure that was Jillian's intent. "You're a goddamn tease," he said, smiling at her.

"So you've said." She kissed his mouth and ran her tongue along his bottom lip. "I might be a tease, but you can always count on me putting out."

A gruff laugh escaped him. "Yeah, you're easy that way."

"Mmm." She moved off his lap and knelt in front of him, then tugged on the waistband of his silk pajama pants. Knowing what she wanted, and *dying* for the same thing, he lifted his hips, enabling her to pull them completely off.

He sat in the dining room chair, completely naked, his erection a solid eight inches thick and straining against his stomach. Pushing his knees apart, she lowered her head, touching her lips to the inside of his thigh, then slowly, leisurely licked her way upward.

"There's more," she murmured huskily, her breath gusting hot and damp on his skin. "Keep looking."

He turned another page and came across a picture of her in that dominatrix get-up she'd worn for him a few weeks ago. She looked amazing in the form-fitting red leather bustier and fuck-me stilettos, with her hair all disheveled around her bare shoulders and a flirty smile curving the corners of her mouth. But it was the leather crop she held in her hands that flooded his mind with the unforgettable images of him being tied to the bed, and how he'd witnessed a whole different side to his wife that night that he never knew existed.

Her fingers gripped his shaft, stroking his length while Jillian's other hand fondled his taut balls as he looked at the seductive pictures of her. He felt like a teenager again, flipping through a Penthouse magazine while jacking off to photos of half-naked women. Except it was his wife who was unraveling him—licking the pre-cum from the swollen head before sucking him deep into her warm, wet mouth—and *holy fuck*, the culmination of both sensory reactions created one of the most erotic, mind-blowing experiences of his life.

Concentrating on anything but erupting like a volcano took extreme effort and control as she wrapped her silky tongue around his cock and slowly withdrew, adding another level of pleasure to her skillful blow job before deep-throating him once again.

A tremor ran through him, and he braced his feet on the floor and gritted his teeth to keep from exploding in her mouth, just as he reached the middle of the album. And just like an actual centerfold spread, he had to turn the book sideways and open another page, revealing a full featured pin-up of Jillian that literally stole the breath from his lungs. She was laying in the middle of their bed on her back, mostly naked and back-dropped by rumpled silky sheets the color of deep amethyst—a stunning contrast to her rich brown hair and smooth, creamy complexion.

Her hair was spread out around her head, her back was arched, and one arm was crossed over her bare breasts, barely concealing them. Her torso and stomach were bare, as were her thighs and endlessly long legs. A swath of purple silk draped across her hips, the only bit of modesty in an otherwise intoxicating photograph. Her other hand disappeared beneath that thin strip of sheet, giving the illusion that she was touching herself in a very intimate way.

The picture itself was seductive and suggestive, but it was the euphoric look on her face that riveted him. Her eyes were closed, her lips slightly parted, appearing as though she was in the throes of ecstasy as she pleasured herself. This was his wife at her most confident and uninhibited, yet vulnerable in a way that humbled him, because she'd given him something so incredibly private and erotic and personal.

Between the arousing photos and Jillian's talented mouth working his cock, pure, unadulterated lust bolted through him, the rush so hot and deep he knew he was on the verge of combusting. There were so many more pages still left to see, but right now he wanted the real Jillian, flesh and blood and the clasp of her soft, warm sheathe enveloping him, instead of her mouth.

Setting the book on the table to finish looking at later, he wrapped his fingers in her hair and pulled her lips free of his cock. "Ah, shit," he groaned, both relieved and disappointed by the loss of all that silky, suctioning heat. "You need to stop. That feels too damned good."

Her lips were parted and glistening, her gaze heavy-lidded and beguiling as she looked up at him from between his spread legs. "Then let me finish."

"Not tonight," he said, his voice gruff. "I

want to be balls deep inside you when I come."

She laughed softly. "Look at you, being all romantic," she teased, and rose to her feet so she was standing in front of him. "How about you unwrap me first?"

She toyed with the ribbons lacing up the right side of her negligee, from hip to just under her arm. Reaching out, he placed his hand just above her knee then gradually skimmed his palm up her smooth thigh until his fingers disappeared into the slit of the gown and his thumb grazed the soft, very wet lips of her sex.

Ahhh, no panties, just as he'd thought.

She swallowed back a moan and pushed her hips against his hand, clearly wanting a deeper, firmer touch. Not yet ready for her to come, either, he left her aching and instead tugged on the ribbons securing the two panels of black silk fabric. He unlaced the criss-cross pattern until he held the long, thin strip of material in his hand, and the sides of her negligee fluttered open.

He glanced up at Jillian, his lips twitching with a wicked smile. "You do realize how handy this ribbon is, don't you?" Thoughts of tying her hands behind her back while he fucked her danced in his head, tempting him.

She rolled her eyes and put him in his place in a way only his wife could. "You don't always have to be the one in control, Dean. Tonight, I'd prefer mutual pleasure. And I want to be able to touch you."

"Fine." He exhaled a begrudging sigh that was completely feigned and dropped the ribbon to the floor. "Next time, then."

"You are such a little *boy* sometimes," she chided, clearly amused by his indignation for not getting his way.

There was no point in denying her claim. "Now take off the rest of the gown so I can look my fill of you."

With a shrug of her shoulders, she let both straps fall down her arms, and the silky fabric slithered down her body until it pooled around her feet and she was as naked as he was. The blood heated in his veins as he raked his gaze along the length of her, refueling the pulse of need throbbing in his dick. Her body was lush and curvy and so fucking perfect, and he couldn't wait another second to be inside her.

"Come here and straddle my cock so I can get as deep as possible," he ordered, not caring that he was getting demanding, when he'd promised he'd give his wife romance tonight. Well, tough shit. He wanted her too badly to go slow and sweet.

She moved over his lap, her legs on either side of his thighs, her palms resting on his shoulders. He took his thick, rigid cock in his hand, rubbed the tip along her slick folds, and positioned the burgeoning head right at her entrance. "Take me, baby girl," he said, his voice rough and desperate. "*All* of me, all at once."

She came down on him in one smooth, fluid movement, taking him to the hilt until she was impaled fully on his steel rod. He grabbed her waist and pulled her down even harder, then tilted her hips and thrust upward, so there was absolutely nothing separating the two of them. She shuddered and cried out in surprise, her fingernails digging into his shoulders. He reveled in the sharp bite of pain, as well as that wide-eyed look of hers as she stared down at him.

He couldn't help the smug smile that eased up one side of his mouth. "Does that feel like a *little boy* to you?" he taunted, grinding his groin against hers.

Breathless laughter escaped her. "Okay, I'll admit, that feels like all *man* to me."

"Damn straight," he said, and grunted for emphasis.

She shook her head in playful disbelief. "You're such a braggart."

He chuckled, enjoying the fun, flirtatious banter between them. "It's not bragging when it's the truth."

Finished talking, he gathered both of her breasts in his hands, dipped his head, and laved first one nipple, then the other, before sucking the turgid peak all the way into his mouth. She sighed softly, blissfully, as his tongue licked and swirled, until he unexpectedly bit down on her nipple and tugged hard, knowing he was riding a very fine line between pleasure and torture.

"*Dean!*" She gasped in shock, her entire

body jerking in response to the sharp nip of his teeth once again.

Her pussy clenched around him as he continued to tease and torment her, a positive sign that she liked the twinge of pain despite her paltry protests. She twisted her fingers in his hair to tug him away, but he was relentless, proving that he didn't need to tie her up in order to have his way with her.

She bucked and writhed wildly against him, forcing his cock impossibly deeper with every jerky thrust of her hips. Her head rolled back and her spine arched as she begged and cursed him at the same time . . . to stop, don't stop, *to please make her come*. He increased the suction of his mouth and the pinch of his fingers as she rode him, fast and hard, her lust and need so beautifully unbridled, and holy hell, she was so fucking hot and sexy like this, so irresistible.

Her body tightened around his cock and she screamed as her orgasm tumbled through her, triggering his own release. He finally let go of her breasts, and placing his hands on either side of her face, he brought her lips to his, devouring her mouth in a bone-melting kiss that made her shudder against him. His tongue invaded, owned and possessed, just as his cock filled her and his cum spilled deep inside her tight, convulsing body.

She collapsed against him in a soft, boneless heap, her face buried against his neck and both of them breathing hard.

"Was that pleasure *mutual* enough for you?" He murmured against her ear, uncaring of just how smug he sounded.

A small, amused gust of laughter escaped her. "Not only are you a braggart, but you're arrogant, too."

He grinned, unable to deny her accusation, because, yeah, he was feeling *very* full of himself. "Guilty of both counts."

She sighed, her body relaxing completely as she cuddled against his chest and he gently stroked her bare back with his hands. "That was nice."

He stopped the caress of fingers down her spine and frowned. "Just *nice*?" he asked incredulously. Talk about an ego-deflator.

"Amazing?" She lifted her head from his shoulder, enabling him to see the teasing light glimmering in her eyes.

"Better," he grumbled, and arched a brow, waiting for her to improve her definition.

"Phenomenal?" She bit her bottom lip to keep from laughing.

"Damn straight," he growled, then twisted his fingers in her hair and kissed her, long, hard, and deep. His cock stirred, pulsing with heat and renewed lust as she kissed him back, tongue's tangling, lips sliding, and her hands in his hair, too.

God, what this woman, *his wife*, did to him. He might like being in control and dominant, but she truly had the ability to make him weak when it came to wanting her. She unraveled him, emotionally and physically, and with her, he knew he could let himself go and be a better man for it.

She moaned against his lips and began rocking her hips against his, rubbing and undulating like a nymph, her own desire returning with just as much rising intensity.

Wanting her on a soft bed so he could pound into her like he was dying to, he grabbed her ass in his hands, holding her tight against him as he quickly stood up, keeping their bodies joined.

Startled by the abrupt move, she threw her arms around his neck and wrapped her legs around his waist, clinging to him. "What are you doing?" she said, her voice a squeak of surprise.

He headed toward their bedroom, feeling the slide of his cock inside her every step of the way. "It's our twentieth anniversary, baby. I'm not done with you yet, especially after that *nice* comment of yours. Before the night is through, I want you to see fucking *fireworks*."

Husky, playful laughter filled his ears. "You can certainly give it your best shot."

Reaching their bed, he laid her down on the mattress, pinned her arms above her head and spent the next few hours making good on his promise.

CHAPTER 3

*J*illian couldn't remember feeling so excited and nervous at the same time—excited to see what The Players Club was all about, and nervous about what to expect once she and Dean arrived at the massive, sprawling mansion. Ever since accepting her husband's invitation on their anniversary, her anticipation had grown, and tonight was finally the night they'd step outside the boundaries of their own personal playroom and explore more public, forbidden temptations.

Exhaling a deep breath to calm the butterflies in her stomach, Jillian glanced in the dresser mirror to check her reflection one last time. Per her husband's request, she was wearing his favorite "little black dress"—a very form-fitting sheath made of shimmering black material that ended mid-thigh. The front had a high neck and long sleeves, giving the illusion of modesty, but the low-cut, backless design made it impossible for her to wear a bra, and the clinging material molded to her full breasts in a way he loved. The only thing she wore beneath were a pair of black lace panties.

As she waited for Dean to finish up in the bathroom, she slid her feet into a pair of strappy black stilettos then retrieved a velvet lined jewelry box from the safe in the closet and brought it back to her dresser. She opened the box, a reminiscent smile touching her lips as she viewed the long strand of pink-hued freshwater pearls that Dean had given to her a few months ago—and felt a flush of warmth cascade along her skin when she recalled exactly what he'd done with those pearls when they'd returned from dinner that long ago evening.

"Don't put those on," Dean said from behind her before she could lift the necklace from where it was nestled in black satin.

She glanced over her shoulder at him, her entire body going soft and warm as she took in her sexy, gorgeous husband in a tailored pair of black slacks and a black silk shirt that enhanced his dark, good looks. "Why not? This necklace goes so well with this dress."

"Don't get me wrong, I love that pearl necklace and its many uses," he said, the heat in his gray eyes telling her that his memories of that night were just as vivid and erotic as her own. "But I have an anniversary gift for you."

She frowned in confusion and turned around to face him. "I thought tonight's invitation to The Players Club was my gift."

"The invitation was for *us*," he clarified, and handed her a flat, square jewelry box with a familiar jeweler's name imprinted on top. His smile was boyishly charming. "I think after putting up with me for twenty years you deserve something special and just for *you*. I would have given this to you the night of our anniversary, but I had it custom made and it wasn't quite ready."

She absently caressed her fingers over the soft velvet lining the top of the box, certain he'd paid a small fortune for whatever was inside. "You didn't have to do this, you know."

He pressed his fingers to her lips, and she was glad she hadn't put any lipstick on yet. "I wanted to, and not a word out of your mouth about the cost, either," he added, seemingly reading her thoughts. "I can afford to buy my wife nice things, and I shouldn't be denied that pleasure."

Knowing he meant what he said, that spoiling her was something he truly enjoyed, she pushed the lid open and was nearly blinded by the brilliant sparkle of diamonds. Lots and lots of diamonds and way too many for her to even count. She stared in shock at the necklace—both dazzled and stunned by the three rows of high quality, flawless stones that would encircle her neck. An elegant design of a D and J intricately joined was at the center of the breath-taking piece.

"Holy . . ." she swallowed back the unladylike curse word and raised her wide-eyed gaze to Dean, her heart beating like a drum in her chest. "Dean, this is too much!"

He rolled his eyes at her protest, as if he'd expected it. "Too damn bad. It's a custom design, paid for and non-refundable. Not another word out of you, unless you'd like to break in the new ball gag I bought but we haven't used yet," he teased in a soft threat as he lifted the piece of jewelry from the box. "Now turn around so I can put it on you."

Even as she wondered about his ball gag comment, she did as he asked and lifted her hair so he could put the jewelry around her neck and secure the clasp. Standing behind her, he looked over her shoulder and into the mirror reflecting both of their images.

"It's perfect, just like you," he murmured, strumming the tips of his fingers down her bare spine.

His light caress made her shiver and her nipples tighten against the fabric of her dress. The look in his eyes was so tender for a man with such a tough facade, and that emotion completely melted her heart. She touched her fingers to the smooth diamonds, which fit closely around her neck like a choker. "I truly love it. Especially our entwined initials." *Especially that.*

"I designed it myself." He smiled, clearly proud of himself. "I have one more surprise for you before we go."

He went to his dresser and withdrew another box, this one small and white with no indication of what might be inside. A slight smirk canted the corner of his mouth as he gave her the gift. "I thought we'd make tonight more . . . interesting."

His smooth, seductive drawl was like a caress in and of itself and her stomach suddenly tumbled with awareness as she opened the box, revealing a small, egg-shaped vibrator. The sex toy was compact, about two inches in diameter and length, and textured with at least two dozen nubs on the purple silicone sleeve encasing it.

"It's a pleasure orb," Dean said, his eyes twinkling wickedly. "It slips inside of you, it can vibrate, and it just so happens to come with a wireless remote. "Very clever and discreet, don't you think?"

She swallowed hard, knowing exactly why he'd given her the present *now*, instead of surprising her with it one night in their playroom. "And you think I'm going to let you put that thing in me, then walk around with it buzzing inside me tonight?"

His grin turned positively sinful. "Of course you are," he said presumptuously, before putting the remote in his pocket and plucking the toy from the box. "Now lift the hem of your dress so I can do the honors."

"Your arrogance knows no bounds," she grumbled, just because her husband was way too used to getting his way. "Fine, I'll let you put the vibrator inside me, but do *not* abuse your power with the remote."

He just smiled, oozing way too much bad boy charm. His non-verbal reply told her that he had no intention of following her orders, that he'd do *what* he wanted, *when* he wanted. The man was absolutely incorrigible, and goddamn irresistible.

Denying him was impossible, especially when she knew that what he wanted would turn them both on. Setting the box on the dresser, she pulled her dress up to her waist and he stepped closer, his gaze holding hers—brimming with pure alpha heat. He touched the egg to her belly, just above the waistband of her panties, and she shivered as the device started to hum very softly.

"Feet wide apart," he commanded softly.

The assertive note to his voice made her melt deep inside, made her wet with desire, forcing her to admit just how much she loved this more sexually dominant side to Dean's personality. She braced her stilettos apart, opening her legs and allowing him all the access he needed. She was already starting to pant, her anticipation so strong as she waited for the vibrator to make contact with her clit so she could come.

He slipped his hand, and that thrilling orb, into her panties and along her smooth, bare mound. Her thighs were shaking by the time he reached her soft nether lips, her sex aching with need.

"You're already dripping wet," he

murmured, triumphant with the discovery. "You want to come, don't you, baby girl?"

She nodded jerkily as he let the vibrator brush across her clit like a flickering kiss. "Yes, please." *And what a lovely start to the evening that would be.*

He sighed in disappointment, and deliberately kept the caress of the toy light and fleeting, which only served to make her even more sensitive. "There's that impatience again," he said, reminding her of times in the past when he'd chastised her for not having any restraint—for being greedy and wanting an orgasm *now*, instead of allowing the pleasure to build, which he preferred.

Knowing that Dean always got his way, there was no doubt in her mind that he was going to tease and torment her with the orb, and keep her climax at bay until *he* decided he was ready to give it to her—both a thrilling and frustrating prospect.

She gasped as he pushed the device inside her body and the oval object nestled right along her g-spot. The soft, pulsating sensation fluttered against the sensitive lining of her sheath, and even when Dean withdrew his hand and she was able to squeeze her legs together again, no amount of pressure could relieve the too elusive need for satisfaction, not unless he increase the speed of the vibrator.

And the rogue knew it, too.

She shoved her dress back down into place. Her body was cruising just below climaxing, like an itch begging to be scratch but was just beyond her reach. It made her nerve endings spark with heat, made her nipples tight and hard. She was tempted to touch herself and enjoy a quick orgasm—because if she didn't, he was going to keep her completely distracted with his new toy.

Reaching out a hand, she cupped the hard length of his cock straining against the fly of his pants, gratified to see that he was just as affected. Then an idea popped into her head. "How about a quick blow job in exchange for my orgasm before we leave?" It seemed like more than a fair trade to her.

His gaze flickered with amusement. "Who knew you had such bartering skills?"

She was beginning to feel a bit desperate with the faint strum of the vibrator taunting her with what her body craved. "I just know that I'm going to be on edge all night if you don't let me come now, at least once."

He gave her a shameless smile. "That will make two of us, and just think how good it's going to be when I finally do let you come."

"Bastard," she said, meaning it in the most loving way possible. "I should make you wear your vibrating cock ring so you know what this feels like."

He chuckled. "Not gonna happen, sweetheart. Not tonight, anyways."

"Then how about I just give myself an orgasm," she said, and slid her hand back under her dress so that she could press her fingers against her clit. Relief was only a few strokes away.

He grabbed her wrist in a tight grip and jerked her hand away. "Don't you dare," he growled, his eyes turning a dark, threatening shade of slate. "If you do anything to make yourself come before I allow you to, your ass is going to be so pink and sore you won't be able to sit for a week."

She shivered, imagining how erotic it would feel for him to spank her while the orb thrummed inside her. The thought made her breathless. "Then turn the damn thing off and give me a break. I'm so freakin' aroused I can't think straight!"

His hand disappeared into his pants pocket, and second later the toy stopped vibrating, *thank God*.

"There you go, for now." He arched a dark, mocking brow. "Better?"

She exhaled, grateful for the blessed reprieve, though her body was still humming deep inside, even without the constant stimulation. "Much better, you sadist," she said, only half-joking.

"Oh, you have no idea," he murmured, taking no offense to her comment as he strolled into the bathroom and washed his hands, then returned a moment later. "Ready to go?"

Jillian nodded, as ready as she'd ever be.

Five minutes later they were in Dean's Aston Martin, with him at the wheel as he drove them toward their destination for the evening.

The Players Club was tucked away in the hills of Fallbrook and overlooked the city, the vast, multi-acre estate protected by an impenetrable iron gate that only opened after approval from one of the two guards on duty. From there, a long, winding driveway led the way even higher, the smooth, paved roadway fringed by impeccably landscaped grounds that were green, lush, and illuminated by low profile Malibu lighting.

The road came to an end at an enormous circular drive, where they were greeted by a valet who whisked away Dean's car and left them standing in front of the monstrous, majestic mansion that was three stories tall and so incredibly wide it took up most of the mountainside. The architecture was Mediterranean in style, with arches and columns, and stone and tile detailing. From the outside, there was nothing to indicate that this gorgeous, luxurious house was a club that catered to all sorts of sexual adventures and taboo desires.

At the realization that they were actually about to step inside The Players Club and indulge in some of those kinks, her stomach did one of those slow tumbles that encompassed both excitement and a bit of nervousness.

As if completely in tune to her emotions, Dean took her hand in his and gave it a gentle squeeze. "Are you absolutely sure about this?" he asked, his voice low and rife with understanding. "Because if you're uncertain about going inside, it's not too late to change your mind."

Her husband was such a bold, domineering man in most aspects of his life, but it was times like this, when he exposed that rare, sensitive side that he kept so deeply buried that Jillian fell deeper in love with him. It meant everything to her that he took her feelings into consideration, that even now that they'd been admitted into the estate he was still willing to turn right back around and leave at her say so.

But despite her nerves, that wasn't what

she wanted. "I'm good," she said, her reply completely honest. "It's just a little fear of the unknown."

The tips of his fingers touched her face and skimmed along her jaw. "If there is anything at all that makes you uncomfortable once we're inside, just say the word and we're outta there, got it?"

She smiled, that bit of security making all the difference. "Thank you."

Dean tucked her hand possessively in the crook of his arm as they headed up the stairs and into the open courtyard, complete with a four-tiered marble fountain. The double front doors to the mansion were giant-sized and inlaid with beveled glass, and just as they arrived they opened. A pretty blonde haired woman greeted them, introducing herself as Cindy, one of the club's hostesses for the evening.

After double-checking to make sure they were on the approved list, she led them into a large, spacious room that had been transformed into a bar and lounge, where most singles and couples mingled before venturing off to various areas of the mansion. Per the dress code for the lounge area, everyone was dressed decently—the women in nice outfits that covered all the essentials and the men in slacks and shirts, as if they were attending a normal cocktail party and not hanging out in a sex club.

The vibe was upscale, yet intimate. Elegant, yet seductive. Most everyone seemed familiar and friendly with each other as they conversed and socialized, giving Jillian the impression that they'd been here before and already knew the ropes, so to speak. Considering the exclusivity of the club, she and Dean were probably only a few of the first-timers there, but the atmosphere was warm and welcoming. As they strolled into the lounge, inviting smiles were cast their way, as well as interested glances from both men and women.

"There's Mac and a few of my guys," Dean said, and with his big, warm hand splayed against the small of her bare back, he escorted her in that direction.

As they approached the circle of men, Mac glanced up, saw them, and offered her a wolfish grin. The man was an outrageous flirt, even with her, and never missed an opportunity to let all that sexy charm work to his advantage. He was also like a brother to Dean, and there was no shortage of ribbing and rivalry between the two, with her sometimes caught in the middle.

Ignoring Dean completely, Mac stepped up to her, grabbed her hand, and kissed her on the cheek. "I keep waiting for you to realize what a schmuck Dean is and run away with me," he said, a teasing light in his dark blue eyes that reminded her of rich sapphires. "Care to be persuaded this evening?"

She bit her lower lip to keep from laughing. Mac was truly the one man who could talk to her so boldly and actually get away with it.

"Back off, Romeo," Dean said before she could issue her own response. "She prefers quality over quantity."

"Why don't we let *her* be the judge of that?" Mac replied smoothly, just to antagonize Dean a bit more.

Dean scowled at him. "Don't make me

kick your ass *here*, in front of all these nice people, and get your membership revoked."

"Next time, then," Mac said, winking at her. He turned to the other two men standing just behind him, who'd been watching the exchange with amusement, and introduced them. "You remember Logan and Sawyer, don't you?"

Jillian nodded. She'd met both of them, and others, at a fund-raiser they'd all attended a few months ago. Both men were extremely good looking and built like The Rock. "Nice to see you two again."

"Same here," they replied in unison.

Despite these men working for Dean, there was no awkwardness between any of them. Clearly, they were all comfortable here at The Players Club, and with the situation, which made everything so much easier for Jillian.

"I was just going to head to the bar to get a drink," Mac said, inclining his head toward her. "Would you like to come with me? These boys have a few work related things to discuss before the fun begins."

"Sure." She slipped her hand into his extended arm. "I'd love a glass of wine."

Mac led her away, and from behind her she heard Dean say in a low growl, "Keep your eyes off my wife's ass," to one of the other two men in the group.

"Sorry, sir," Logan said, sounding startled that he'd been caught.

Mac chuckled, having heard the conversation, too. "I have to admit, *I'm* having a hard time not looking at your ass in that dress. You look fantastic, by the way."

She thanked him with a smile. "Dean and I have established a look but don't touch rule that goes both ways, so he shouldn't be snapping at one of his guys when I've seen plenty of the women in here staring at him, too."

"He's just marking his territory, as I would if you were with me," he said as they reached one end of the bar. "Speaking of Dean marking his territory, that's a stunning collar you're wearing. It pretty much guarantees that any man looking at you knows you're taken."

Startled by his descriptive word, and

what it implied, her fingers fluttered to the diamond choker encircling her throat. *"Collar?"*

"Did I say collar?" He looked at her with way too much innocence for a very experienced man who knew the in's and out's of BDSM. "I meant *necklace*."

No, she was certain he'd meant collar, and realized that was probably Dean's purpose, too. Her husband might be okay with other men looking, but the diamonds fitted tightly around her neck made a clear statement that she was taken—his quiet stamp of ownership.

The bartender arrived, and she ordered a glass of white wine and Mac asked for his standard Johnnie Walker Black. Just as the bartender turned away to prepare their drinks, Jillian gasped and literally jumped in place as an unexpected shocking sensation rippled deep inside her body, then settled into a slow, pleasurable hum against her g-spot. She clutched the edge of the mahogany bar, and just in time swallowed the moan that rose into her throat, catching the purely sexual sound before it could escape.

Mac glanced at her, a slight frown of concern marring his brows. "Did something startle you?"

She was going to *kill* her husband. With effort, she tried to act normal, to pretend that she didn't have a pleasure orb stimulating sensitive nerve endings and wreaking havoc with her concentration. "I'm . . . I'm fine." She was so breathless she could barely talk.

Mac didn't look completely convinced, but said nothing more. Their drinks arrived, and she took a big gulp of her wine, needing a bit of alcohol in her system to relax. She shuddered as the toy continued rubbing and shaking against her inner walls. Mac noticed her inability to stand still, and suddenly appeared very amused, his gaze much too perceptive.

"Dean must have got himself a new toy to play with," he said, and grinned.

Jillian's face flushed crimson, confirming Mac's guess without saying a word. "I plead the fifth, and you are absolutely *shameless* for even going there."

"I've been called much worse, and you should know by now that I'm about as bad as they come," he replied with humor as he escorted her back toward Dean—who had his hand in his pocket and a smirk on his face.

The guys completed their conversation, while Jillian finished her wine, watching as couples paired up and left the lounge area in pursuit of other adventures. Logan broke away from their group to approach an attractive brunette, then Sawyer joined two women who'd been blatantly eyeing him, clearly angling for double the pleasure.

Jillian shifted on her feet and pressed her thighs together, barely able to maintain her composure with the vibrator humming so illicitly inside her—just enough to keep her on that fine edge of need. Dean chatted with Mac a few moments longer, before Mac finally took pity on her and decided to be on his way, too.

"Looks like your wife is getting anxious to check out the rest of the club," Mac teased, making a not-so-subtle reference to just how fidgety she was. "My date for the evening just walked in, so you two have fun, and don't do anything I wouldn't do."

Which left them wide-open with possibilities, Jillian was certain.

Mac stepped up to her and brushed his lips across her cheek in a platonic kiss. "Just relax and enjoy yourself," he murmured into her ear. "That's what we're all here for."

She watched him saunter away with masculine grace and way too much sexual confidence, toward a raven haired woman with bombshell curves who greeted him with a familiar smile. They spoke for a few seconds, the woman laughed in sensual delight at something Mac said, and a moment later they were gone, too.

Dean took the empty wine glass from her and set it on a nearby table. "Ready for me to give you a tour of the place?" he asked.

"You?" She narrowed her gaze suspiciously at her husband. "What do you know about the inside of The Players Club?"

"Enough." He shrugged, much too

nonchalantly. "I stopped by yesterday afternoon for a private, first-timer's tour. I wanted to know exactly what to expect, and I needed to set up a few things for tonight's fantasy."

"Oh." That he'd given this evening's activities that much thought, to the point that he'd made certain arrangements prior to them arriving, amped up her curiosity. "You can do that?"

"Yes." He placed his hand on her lower back and guided her out of the lounge. "Members can reserve certain rooms ahead of time, depending on their interest or kink, and I had something particular in mind for you and I. But first, let's look around together."

They strolled back into the grand entry hall, where other people were also milling about and heading in different directions. The enormous chandelier hanging from the ceiling cast prisms of light around the room as they stopped before a split staircase with two directional signs: to the right for public viewing rooms, and to the left for private rooms. Another stairway led down another flight of stairs with a sign designating that area "The Dungeon".

"The Dungeon is probably a little more hard-core than we want to venture into, at least on our first night here," Dean said before she could ask what *that* part of the mansion entailed. "Lots of whips, chains, and more on the sado-masochistic side of things."

Admittedly, Jillian was beginning to enjoy a little pain with her pleasure, but her husband was right . . . she wasn't quite ready to venture down such an extreme path on their first visit to The Player's Club.

They ascended the stairs, veered off to the right, and spent the next half hour exploring the open, public, viewing areas—where you could either be a voyeur or exhibitionist. Dean refused to turn off the pleasure orb still vibrating inside her, and the physical stimulation coupled with the visual titillation heightened every one of her five senses as they watched all sorts of sexual vices play out before them: couples fucking, women on women getting it on, orgies, and light BDSM just to name a few of the milder acts.

They passed through rooms decorated in themes, complete with costumes, where people acted out their fantasies for everyone to watch. All around them was the scent of sex, the sound of sex . . . heavy breathing. Moans. The slap of flesh against flesh. Gasps of pleasure. It was sensory overload, like the hottest form of foreplay, and she was drenched as a result.

Dean stopped her at a window that looked into a room where two men were pleasuring a woman—or rather, she was letting them do as they pleased to *her*. Dean moved behind her, hands on her waist as he pressed the thick, straining length of his cock bulging the fly of his slacks up against her ass . . . just like one of the guys in the viewing room was fucking the woman who was on her hands and knees, while the woman sucked the other man's cock.

Lust sizzled through Jillian as Dean ground himself harder against her backside, his breath hot against her ear, the hum of the vibrator ramping up her arousal and making her desperate for some kind of relief.

"Do you like watching those two men having their way with that woman?" he murmured huskily, clearly just as turned on by the sight. "Are you imagining yourself as that woman, wondering what it would feel like to give and receive pleasure at the same time?"

Oh, yes, she *imagined*, and that fantasy liquefied her. Her nipples turned hard and tight as the trio in the enclosed room continued fucking and sucking, and she whimpered in response and thrust her hips back against Dean's, grinding against his stiff erection.

His breath exhaled on a groan, and a moment later the vibrator inside her kicked up a notch, jolting her entire body with the shocking sensation. Jillian's eyes nearly rolled into the back of her head, and her knees would have completely given out on her if Dean hadn't wrapped a strong arm around her waist to anchor her body to his. His free hand slid around to the front of her dress and slipped beneath the hem, skimming upward until his fingers dipped beneath the elastic band of her panties and stroked her wet flesh.

She bit her bottom lip to keep from crying out at the contact, and without thinking she braced her stilettos further apart, giving him complete access to her.

"Keep watching," he demanded in a rough whisper as his fingers brushed over her pulsing clit and tugged on the engorged flesh, taunting her just like the orb teased and tormented her deep inside. "Keep imagining."

She couldn't do anything *but* watch and imagine, the fantasy so potent her mouth went dry and moisture rushed between her legs. A part of her brain told her she ought to be mortified for being so uninhibited. They were in a public area. There were people nearby, behind them, probably even watching as Dean's fingers worked their magic and promised satisfaction. But she didn't care. They were both still fully clothed and her body's demands over-ruled all common sense, especially when her husband knew exactly how to touch her to make her shatter into a million pieces.

In that crazy moment, she let go of everything—her modesty, her reserve, her embarrassment—and knowing that Dean would catch her in his strong arms she embraced the rush of ecstasy pulsing in her veins. Her head fell back onto his shoulder, a mewling sound escaping her throat as her body convulsed with a pleasure so intense she nearly blacked out.

When she finally regained her senses he was holding her, the arm banded around her waist keeping her upright. Gradually, their surroundings came back into focus, along with the knowledge of what she'd just done in front of strangers. Heat swept across her cheeks, the warmth spreading all the way to the tips of her ears.

Dean's face was buried against the side of her neck, his breath damp and heavy against her skin. "That was so fucking hot," he rasped as he removed his hand from beneath her dress and straightened the hem, keeping her perfectly, decently covered.

She felt him shift behind her, and a few seconds later the toy inside her stopped vibrating so that she could relax more fully. He withdrew something from his pocket, the silky material brushing along her arm as he brought the item up in front of her to see.

"Now we get to the really good part of the evening," he said, his voice low, soft and seductive against the shell of her ear. "I'm going to put this blindfold on you and I'm going to push you past anything we've ever done before. I want you to trust me to take you there in a way that's safe and secure, okay?"

A frisson of excitement coursed through her as she nodded. His words were vague and gave nothing away, yet she knew whatever he had planned would be hot, thrilling, and *daring*. He slipped the black, silk mask over her eyes, plunging her into compete darkness—and a part of her was grateful for the blindfold so she didn't have to look anyone in the eye after what they'd just done.

"I *always* trust you," she said with

conviction and certainty. It was the one thing she could always count on when it came to Dean.

"Tonight is going to test that trust in ways that will shock you," he murmured as he strummed his warm fingers down her bare back. "And I need you to remember that I wouldn't do anything to hurt you, or *us*. However, if things get too intense for you, all you need to do is say our safe word and it all ends immediately."

She swallowed hard. That he had to qualify this evening's adventure with such a warning had her imagination spinning in all sorts of dark, decadent, wanton directions. "Fair enough."

CHAPTER 4

*D*ean secured an arm around her back, tucked her against his side, and led her . . . *somewhere*. Jillian had never had a good sense of direction, and being blindfolded completely threw her coordinates off balance. All she could do was let him guide her while listening to the various sounds of the club—laughter, groans, and even screams of pleasure—all amplified by the loss of her vision. She felt as though she was being led through a maze, and a short while later she heard a door close and Dean released her so that she was standing alone, the faint scent of vanilla and cinnamon wrapping around her. Wherever they were, it was completely silent, except for Dean's footsteps as he moved around the room.

"Where are we?" she asked.

"That will be your one and only question before we get started," he said, the commanding tone of his voice letting her know that he was now in charge, that the dominant alpha male that she loved had come out to play. "Tonight, you're mine, to do with as I please. Going forward, I will be the one asking questions and making demands, and you will obey and reply with *sir*. There will be punishments for insubordination and consequences for hesitating when I tell you to do something. Do you understand?"

"Yes . . . Sir," she added quickly, almost forgetting the word.

"As for where we are, we're in a small, comfortable room that I reserved and stocked with a few items to use tonight, like this new leather paddle," he said, and followed that up with a firm smack against what sounded like his palm. "There's a large glass window in front of where you're standing, so anyone can watch us, just like we watched those two men fuck that woman. We haven't even started and we're already drawing a nice little crowd."

Oh, God. Her stomach did a tiny somersault. She wasn't sure how she felt about being on the *other side* of the viewing glass, of allowing strangers to get off on her and Dean's pleasure. She'd never been an exhibitionist, she certainly didn't have a model figure to flaunt, but there was safety and comfort in wearing the blindfold—as if she couldn't see them, they didn't really exist. She had to think that way, or else she'd totally lose her nerve.

"Take off your dress and your panties," he ordered.

The brusque command took her off guard, and she hesitated a fraction too long for Dean's liking. He smacked her bottom with the wide, leather paddle, and even through the material of her dress the sting was enough to make her yelp in surprise.

"Do it *now*," he said in a harsh tone. "Or

the second swat will be twice as hard and on your bare ass."

Gathering up her courage, she drew the neckline of the dress down, along with the sleeves, and stripped off the garment as quickly as possible before she changed her mind. She did the same with her underwear, until the only three things she was wearing were her stilettos, the diamond choker around her neck, and the soft, silky mask. Her skin felt warm and flushed as she imagined dozens of eyes taking in her less than perfect figure—her full breasts, the soft curve of her stomach, the flare of her hips. She kept her thighs pressed together, and it was all she could do not to cover herself with her hands because she knew that would earn her another searing spank from her husband's paddle.

"You are so fucking sexy," Dean murmured, as he trailed his fingers along the seam of her thighs, over her bare mound, to her belly, making her shiver at his touch, while at the same time soothing her anxiety and making her melt with his sensual praise. "Absolute perfection. Every single inch of you."

He slowly circled around her, one hand caressing her breast. "Your tits are lush and perfectly shaped, your nipples like hard cherry candies that I can't wait to suck on."

She couldn't wait, either. The tips were so rigid they hurt.

Standing behind her now, he skimmed his palm over her bottom, gently squeezing the flesh in his hand. "Your ass is still nice and pert, and we both know how much I enjoy that soft bit of cushion when I'm fucking you from behind."

She heard the faint flicker of amusement in his voice, a shared intimate moment between them that quickly dissipated when he stroked a hand up her thigh and pushed his fingers in between, where she was wet and silky soft. "And then there's your legs, so long and slender and smooth. Every man in that room is imagining them spread open in invitation so they can see what a pretty cunt you have."

Her heart beat crazy-fast in her chest,

and she wondered how far he intended to take all this. *Trust me*, he'd said, and she exhaled a breath and clung to those comforting words.

She heard him walk away and pick something up that jangled, then returned to stand in front of her. "Give me your hands," he demanded.

She lifted her arms, extending her hands out in front of her. A few seconds later he had both of her wrists secured in leather cuffs, and as she put her arms back down to her sides she felt the heavy weight of a clasp attached to the bindings.

Next, he urged her legs a few inches apart and wrapped a thick leather band of some sort around her upper thigh that felt like a belt, and buckled it in place snug and tight, then repeated the procedure on her other thigh. Once those were in place, he clipped the wrist cuffs to the ones around her thighs, effectively keeping her arms confined to sides.

He tugged on the bindings to make sure they were secure, and excitement and apprehension clashed inside of Jillian.

There would be no covering herself, or touching him, or using her hands to stop him from doing something shocking to her.

He'd taken away her sense of sight, and now her ability to touch. Ultimately, the blindfold and restraints enslaved her to him, made her both vulnerable and submissive to her husband, and gave him all the control. Much to her own surprise, the thought of other people watching her, and Dean, was suddenly becoming a very heady, exhilarating mind game that gave her a bit of a thrill.

The only way she was going to enjoy any of this was to shed *all* her inhibitions and open herself to the possibilities and pleasure that inevitably followed when she allowed Dean free rein with both her mind and body. Giving him her complete trust and faith enabled Jillian to clear her head of any embarrassment or shame and experience desire and passion at its most potent.

She was so lost in her thoughts that the sudden touch of Dean's mouth on her breast made her gasp in surprise. His soft, wet tongue trailed down the slope to the stiff crest, followed by the strong pull of his mouth on her nipple, and the sharp nip of his teeth that felt like a jolt through her entire body. He shifted to the other breast, making the second nipple just as hard, then with a final flick of his tongue the sensation was gone . . . replaced seconds later by an unmerciful pinch on each nub as he attached some kind of contraption to her nipples.

Instantly, a path of fire zinged between her breasts and her clit, and she moaned, long and low as desire and need coiled tight inside her.

"Those nipple clamps look so fucking gorgeous on you," Dean murmured, his voice gruff with satisfaction and arousal. "That bite of pain makes the pleasure hotter, more intense, doesn't it?"

She was so overloaded with sensation she could only manage a whimper in response.

He smacked her ass with the leather paddle, searing her bare flesh with yet another form of stimulation. "Answer me when I ask you a question," he growled ominously.

Her mind was spinning, her pulse racing, her body liquefying from the pleasure/pain he was inflicting. "Yes, sir," she replied breathlessly.

"Now, I want you on your knees," he ordered as he wrapped warm, strong fingers around her upper arm to help her down since she had no use of her hands, until she was kneeling on a soft cushion of some sort.

"Perfect," he murmured, and stroked his fingers along her jawline. "The men in the other room are getting so fucking hard watching how well you obey me, and now they get to see what a talented mouth you have." His thumb skimmed across her bottom lip, then dipped inside, and she automatically licked the pad of his finger.

He exhaled a hiss of breath as his hand fell away. A moment later the pleasure orb still nestled inside of her began a light, sensual hum, just enough to bring those nerve endings back to a heightened level of awareness. Her sex throbbed, and the tips of her breasts tightened even more beneath the pinch of the clamps.

"You may not come," he said, that deep, authoritative tone to his voice magnifying the tingles rippling over her skin as the echo of his zipper lowering rang in her ears. "This is all for *me*, not you. Open your mouth, baby girl. Show everyone how much you love sucking my cock."

She licked her lips before parting them, suddenly eager to do exactly as he asked, to take him to the brink and make him wild. It was the only power and leverage she had over him, and she planned to use it to her advantage.

His fingers slid into her hair, then curled around the nape of her neck in a gentle but firm grip as he guided her forward. He pushed the plump crown of his erect penis into her mouth, and she dragged her tongue across the crest then sucked just on that swollen head, savoring the salty-musky taste of his pre-cum, and teasing him in the process.

He swore beneath his breath and twisted his fingers tighter in her hair so that her scalp prickled, adding another element of pain that felt oh-so-good. "Take *all* of me," he commanded, and pushed deeper into her mouth, giving her no choice but to accept every last inch of him until tip of his cock pressed against the back of her throat.

She managed a convulsive swallow as he remained buried to the hilt, and she felt a shudder wrack through him. Having that little bit of power over her husband was intoxicating considering he had her blindfolded and restrained, but it didn't last long. He withdrew, then pushed back in, fucking her mouth in long, slow, steady strokes that eventually grew rougher, more demanding.

"So fucking good," he uttered, his voice as rough as steel wool as he continued to thrust, filling her mouth again and again. "Suck me harder . . . *deeper*. Give me what all those men out there want. Make me come with that hot, wet mouth of yours."

His words excited her, and she did everything he asked, losing herself in his dominance, his aggressive demands. She was equally turned on, the vibrator inside her rasping against nerve endings, making her desperate for her own release. Her nipples ached, the heavy knot of desire throbbed incessantly between her legs, but she knew her orgasm wasn't going to happen until Dean allowed it to.

And right now, he was more intent on satisfying his needs and lust, and she doubled her efforts to push him over that edge. She sucked, hard and deep, and he swelled against her tongue so that she felt every ridge of his cock and the pulse of semen beneath the taut skin. Another demanding pull of her mouth and he stiffened, a harsh, primitive sound unraveling from his chest as the hand at the back of her neck tightened, holding her in place as he climaxed with such force she had no other choice but to swallow everything he had to give.

He pulled out of her mouth, giving her the chance to breath, though the relentless hum of the orb kept her body primed and ready . . . a constant, arousing buzz that was driving her insane with the need to climax.

With a gentle touch, he smoothed her

hair away from her face. "You are so amazing," he said, his tone warm and appraising as his fingers trailed over her flushed cheek, right along the edge of the mask covering her eyes. "I've never seen so many envious men before, all of them wishing they were the lucky bastard getting sucked off by you. Most of them were stroking their cocks, or getting blown by their partner while they watched you get me off —you're *that* sexy and desirable."

There was a certain rush in knowing other men found her so enticing, but it was the pride in Dean's voice, along with the fact that she'd pleased him, that brought her the most joy and pleasure.

"Are you ready for me to reward you for being such a good girl?" he asked.

She nodded, much too eagerly, and hoped his *reward* included an orgasm, because she couldn't remember ever wanting or needing one so badly. "Yes, sir."

"Stand up," he said, and helped her to her feet. He guided her a few steps away, then stopped. "There's a chair right behind you. Sit down."

She lowered herself to a flat, hard, wooden surface then leaned back against the rungs of the chair. She sat with her knees pressed together, much too primly considering she was still naked and blindfolded, her hands still manacled to her thighs, and her tight, straining nipples still trapped in those tiny torture/pleasure devices.

"Open your legs," Dean said from right beside her, his breath hot in her ear. "Show all those men in the other room what a pretty, pink pussy you have. How smooth and bare it is, and how soft and wet you are. Make them lust for it."

A hot flush suffused Jillian's entire body, and a moment of uncertainty gripped her. Oh, God, could she really do this, show other men the most intimate parts of her that only Dean had known before this moment? Knowing she only had seconds decide, she separated her thighs a few increments, a paltry attempt that didn't go unnoticed by her husband.

"*Wider*, Jillian," he growled the demand, a thread of warning in his voice just as the leather paddled connected with the tender inner skin of her upper thigh.

She jumped at the unexpected sting of pain that radiated upward, toward her sex, which mingled with the buzz of the orb tingling oh-so-subtly against her g-spot. Swallowing hard, she parted her knees another few inches, unable to bring herself to open them all the way.

Dean sighed heavily, impatiently, and she heard him walk away, then return to where she sat. "Obviously, you're going to need a bit of help to keep those legs spread," he said as he encircled one ankle with a leather cuff, repeated the process around the other, then pushed her knees so far apart she was completely, indecently exposed. He connected the manacles around her ankles to something so unyielding it forced her legs to remain stretched wide apart. Closing them was impossible.

She felt so vulnerable, and another wave of doubts crashed over her again. "Dean?" she whispered in a quivering voice, seeking her husband's reassurance.

"It's a steel spreader bar," he explained huskily, clearly aroused by the sight of her trussed up in said device. He stroked a gentle hand up her calf, calming her. "Are you okay?"

He was giving her the opportunity to use the safe word, to stop everything if she couldn't handle what he was asking her to do. *Trust me*, he'd said. *I wouldn't do anything to hurt you, or us*, he'd promised, and she believed him. He wanted this, had thought about it and planned it out even to the point of knowing he'd need to use a *spreader bar* with her.

"Are you ready to end this, Jillian?" he asked softly, still caressing her lower leg with the strum of his warm, strong fingers. "Because it's about to get a helluva lot more intense."

She shivered at the thought. Everything about this was over-the-top *intense*, but she wanted to see it through, for Dean. And because, yeah, she was curious to know where all this was about to lead. She exhaled a deep breath and relaxed once again, readjusting her mindset so that the tension eased from her body, so that it was all about the pleasure and the forbidden thrill her husband was providing.

"I'm good," she said, and meant it.

"What you are is *perfect*," he said, and she heard the smile in his voice.

He stood up and came around the chair so that he was behind her, his hand gliding gently along her jawline. "So, which one of you men wants a taste of the ripest, sweetest peach, and the finest, richest cream?" he announced to the males in the viewing room. "And yes, my wife's pussy tastes *that* decadent."

Jillian's breath hitched as she realized what he was doing, what he was offering. *Holy shit*. Instinctively, she tried to close her legs to all those hungry eyes on her, but the steel rod prevented her from executing the action.

"Umm, we have quite a few volunteers, not that I'm surprised," he murmured in amusement, his mouth near her ear as he spoke, clearly enjoying the power and control he held over her, over the situation. "There's a man, all by himself. He's been watching you so intently. I'm going to let him come inside, allow him to go down on you, and make you come while I watch."

Her entire body tensed all over again, and her pulse raced with a lick of panic as Dean walked away and she heard the door open, then close . . . then more footsteps toward her.

Oh, God, was he really going to let another man pleasure her while he watched?

Her mind spun, and her heart raced so hard it drowned out any other sounds in the room. Inside, she was shaking, trembling, torn between fear and yes, even excitement, because it was a fantasy she'd entertained before . . . but only in her mind. Never would she have ever believed it would become a reality.

Trust me. I wouldn't do anything to hurt you, or us. She silently repeated those words, chanted them in her head like a mantra as she felt the touch of fingers glide along the inside of her thighs, stroking softly, seductively, over and over again, turning her panic into something more provocative . . . like heated desire.

Not being able to see or touch and being completely restrained stripped away her control, and she gave herself over to this erotic scenario, let herself feel and respond to the brush of fingertips up her spread legs followed by the hot, damp touch of firm, sensual lips on her skin . . . sucking, licking, nibbling toward her pulsing sex.

She bit her bottom lip, which did nothing to contain the moan of pure surrender that escaped her throat. His thumbs parted her slick flesh, exposing her every secret, and she shuddered hard as the rasp of a hot tongue dragged across her sensitive folds.

Her hands tightened into fists at her sides, and her head fell back on a gasp as he slowly laved her mons again before his mouth covered her and his tongue lashed her clit—toying, stroking, inflaming her in a way that was intimately familiar, in a way that only one man knew her body well enough to know what she liked, what turned her on the most, and knew exactly what it took to make her climax . . . or keep her right on the sharp, sweet edge of release.

The eroticism of a stranger fantasy mingled with the safety of reality allowed every last bit of reserve to fall away. Her mind embraced the illusion, as did her body. As the mouth on her sex continued to devour her, the vibrations inside her increased, the pleasure orb fluttering against her inner walls. The dark ache of desire rippled through her blood stream, her orgasm so close, so close . . . and then the mouth and fingers between her thighs were gone and the sensation ebbed.

She panted, whimpered, and tears of frustration leaked from her eyes behind the blindfold. She wanted to curse Dean for leaving her so bereft, but knew that wouldn't change a thing, except earn her another smack of the leather paddle.

"Hang on, baby girl," he said, his voice deep and rough with his own desperate need. She could hear him moving around the room, the sound of him quickly shedding his clothes filling her ears then he was back, helping her to stand for a moment so he could sit behind her on the chair. He wrapped a strong arm around her middle, guiding her back down until the tip of his cock, coated with warm, slick lubricant, slid between the crease of her ass and nestled against her back entrance.

"Tell me you need it," he demanded aggressively as that thick crest slipped inside her a teasing inch. "Beg me to fuck you right now and I will."

She whimpered, far beyond *needing* it. She was delirious with lust and frantic to feel him thrust deep inside her *there*, while the vibrator worked its magic against her g-spot. "Yes, please," she said on a strangled moan, uncaring that strangers watched her submit completely to her husband, and plead wantonly for him to take her. "Please fuck me, *now*."

Gripping her hips, he pulled her down to his lap in one quick motion, her back to his chest. She cried out as his searing width invaded her channel and he filled her with a ruthless, demanding upward thrust that made him grunt against her shoulder. The muscles in her spread thighs clenched and quivered as Dean began pushing in and out of her, stimulating those forbidden nerve endings and making her forget that they had an audience.

His hands came around and unclamped the vices biting into her nipples, and she groaned in relief until he pinched and tugged both tender, sensitive tips between his fingers, sending another shockwave of white-hot pleasure straight down to her sex. The sensation was both agonizing and electric, and she went a little wild, bucking her hips back against his groin . . . the only thing she could manage in her various restraints.

"Oh, fuck, yeah," he gruffed out, clearly enjoying her unbridled thrashing that lodged him deeper and caused a breathtaking friction. But not enough to allow her to come, and that's what she wanted most of all.

He slid a hand down to her pussy, strummed his fingers across her swollen clit and wrapped his other hand tight in her hair. He pulled her head back, arching her body as he flex his own hips, riding her hard and deep. Dominating her like a stallion would a mare—powerful and relentless in his pursuit to claim and possess.

"Tell every one of those men out there that you're *mine*," he rasped into her ear, holding her climax just out of reach until she complied with his order.

"Yes, *yours*," she whimpered, her need a blazing inferno burning her up from the inside out. "Only yours."

He grunted his approval, turned her head toward his and sealed his mouth over hers, taking what he wanted, and all thoughts of being watched vanished from her mind. His kiss was hot and purposeful, his tongue as greedy and aggressive as the fingers plying her clit, as ruthless as the orb humming inside her sheathe, and as fierce as the cock impaling her. He touched her everywhere, filled her everywhere, and the onslaught of unrelenting pleasure had her flying into a million sizzling pieces. She cried out against his lips as the unmerciful orgasm raged on, the maelstrom of ecstasy she achieved absolutely unmatched in that moment.

Behind her, she felt Dean's big body shudder hard as he climaxed at the same time, his unraveling groan of satisfaction vibrating through his chest as he came, too. Utterly spent, and completely boneless, her entire body sagged back against his, the only thing she could do considering her legs and arms were still manacled.

In a haze, she felt Dean shift behind her, then he was carrying her, and she sighed as he laid her down on what she assumed was a soft mattress, and her head settled on a plump pillow.

"I can't believe how lucky I am to have such a passionate wife as you," he murmured huskily as he gently released her ankles from the leather cuffs and spreader bar then unbuckled the restraints around her still quivering thighs—taking care of her in a way that was so tender and sweet. "Thank you for allowing me tonight's fantasy. Your submission and trust is one of the most beautiful things you've ever given me, and I will always treasure that. You mean *everything* to me, baby girl."

His words, so filled with love, made her

own chest tighten with deep emotion. Her skin flushed when she thought about how many people, *strangers*, had witnessed her total surrender to her husband at his most sexual, his most powerful, his true self no longer held back by his fear that he'd hurt her, or scare her with the intensity of his primitive, dominant needs.

"I know I pushed you way beyond your comfort zone tonight, but you were absolutely stunning," he said as he kissed the inside of each of the wrists he released from the leather cuffs before settling onto the bed beside her, his big hand splayed on her bare belly, so warm and comforting. "Are you ready to take a look at your surroundings?"

She honestly wasn't sure if she wanted to look out that window where dozens of people had gotten off on Dean fucking her. Where prying eyes had been privy to the intimacy between them. While she'd definitely enjoyed every erotic, provocative thing her husband had done to her, the blindfold had made it so easy to let go of all those inhibitions and succumb to the pleasure.

But she had to face reality at some point, and she nodded, allowing Dean to remove the black silk mask. It took a moment for her eyes to adjust to the dim lighting, and she turned her head to look around. They were in a small, private bedroom, with an adjoining bathroom. The wooden chair she'd sat in was situated in the center of the room, and she forced her gaze to the wall facing that seat. She frowned when she realized that there wasn't a large window for spectators, and quickly glanced back at Dean, who wore a very sexy, knowing smirk.

"This isn't a viewing room," she said, stating the obvious as her mind replayed all the things they'd just done, and how the thought of being watched had elevated and heightened the thrill. Yet she couldn't deny that a part of her was relieved to discover it had always been just the two of them, no one else.

"No, it's not," he replied, the amusement in his eyes darkening to something more fierce and possessive. "You're mine. I know that some men like to share their wives, but I don't, and I won't, *ever*. No man is going to see you naked, or go down on you, or watch me fuck you. That belongs to *us*."

Her husband wasn't a romantic poet, but his words were the sweetest, most profound that she'd ever heard. "So, you planned all this, and wanted me to believe we were being watched?"

"You liked it," he stated matter-of-factly. "But it was all just a hot fantasy, a heady illusion that turned both of us on. I certainly didn't get us an invitation to The Players Club to try something mundane or vanilla."

She laughed, because lately, there was absolutely nothing mundane or vanilla about her husband and sex. And tonight, he'd provided a way to push sexual limits without compromising the integrity of their marriage in any way.

She rolled to her side so that she was facing him, so that she could finally put her hands on his muscled chest and touch him. "Maybe we can come back and try one of those themed rooms we saw, like the one with the jail cell, and you can dress up as a cop with handcuffs and do all kinds of naughty things to me."

Her suggestion made him chuckle. "Damn, I can hardly wait."

CHAPTER 5

"'d like to welcome Jillian Noble to our Cocktails and Cocks Club, and monthly get together," Raina announced, and raised her lemon drop martini in a toast to their newest member.

Paige, who was wearing a sexy black satin and lace corset and black jeans that accentuated her voluptuous curves, grinned her approval. "And our first married member at that. Considering she just celebrated her twentieth anniversary, we all might learn a thing or two from her."

Jillian laughed and clinked her glass

with the other women who were sitting in Raina's living room, all close friends based on their separate businesses that each one of them helped to promote and support. "Thank you all for the invite. I'm happy to be a part of such an exclusive, private group," she teased, and took a drink of her lemon drop martini, which went down as smooth as sweetened lemonade.

"There's not many women we'd allow to join Cocktails and Cocks, but we all agree that you're a great fit." This came from Kendall, the woman who'd taken the gorgeous boudoir photographs of Jillian for Dean's anniversary gift.

"This is true," Stephanie chimed in, the owner of Fantasy Bedrooms, a business that specialized in creating bedrooms and playrooms that were intimate, sexy, and fun. "Not only have you become a valued customer for each one of us, but you've become a trusted friend, too. That doesn't happen very often. In fact, you're the first person we've asked to join us since we started the club three years ago."

"Thank you," Jillian said, truly flattered. Every one of these women had played a part in helping her to spice up her sex life with Dean, and she was grateful to be able to call them all friends. And this fun club, and this girl-time, was exactly what she needed to relieve some of the restlessness and boredom she was experiencing lately—especially on those nights when Dean worked late, or when he went on a business trip.

She licked a bit of sugar from the rim of her martini glass, her curiosity getting the best of her. "So, I get the cocktail part of your club's name, but why cocks?"

"Because we love everything about them," Summer, Paige's assistant, said, her eyes alight with a naughty gleam. "Unfortunately, we're all going through a dry spell right now, so it's nice to have a friend who can supply us all with the silicone, vibrating kind in the meantime."

"And I do have quite the selection," Raina said proudly of her varied selection of dildos at Sugar and Spice. "But as we all know, nothing compares to the feel and thrusting power of the real deal. So yes, we're all insanely jealous that you're getting cock on a regular basis."

Paige finished the rest of her drink and gave Jillian a pointed looked. "We're also insanely jealous that you got an invitation to The Players Club."

Jillian's mouth opened, then closed again, and she glanced at Raina, the only person she'd confided in about her trip to the private sex club. "You told her?" she asked, feeling her face flush now that her secret was out.

"Wow, twenty years of marriage and you still blush," Stephanie said, laughing. "I bet Dean loves that."

"Sorry." Raina gave her an impish smile that was far from contrite. "It's a hazard of being a part of this group. We share everything and there are no sexual secrets between us. We bare it all, so to speak, and now that you're a sworn in member of Cocktails and Cocks, you're obligated to share all the details with us."

"Yes, you have to let us live vicariously through you." Eyes wide with curiosity, Summer sat forward on the couch, waiting anxiously to hear everything.

"I think a cocktail refill is in order to loosen up that tongue of yours," Paige said, and poured another round of lemon drop martinis from the pitcher on the coffee table. "I want to know if the guys there are hot, and if they have big cocks."

Jillian laughed, quickly getting used to Paige's outrageous mouth. "Oh, yeah, most of them are hung like stallions." Obviously, the alcohol was making her equally outrageous.

Stephanie gaped at her. "Seriously?!"

Jillian figured it was her job to provide a very titillating and provocative mental image for her friends to enjoy. "The guys are gorgeous. Complete, panty-wetting studs." And if she was talking about Mac, Logan, Sawyer, and her husband, it was the truth. All four men were worthy of that description.

Raina touched the back of her hand to

her forehead and feigned a swoon. "Oh, be still my heart. It's been a helluva long time since *any* man has made my panties wet, and that's truly saying something for a woman who owns a sex shop."

"We all need cock," Stephanie declared, and everyone burst out laughing and toasted to the sentiment.

"Tell us more," Summer said to Jillian, her tone eager.

"Well, the mansion is huge and elegant, with all sort of kinky themes and offerings," Jillian went on as she sipped her second lemon drop. "You can watch, or be watched. There are orgies if that's your thing, a dungeon with hardcore BDSM, or private rooms where you can fulfill your own daring fantasies. The place is decadent, that's for sure."

"I'm emerald-green with envy," Raina said on a sigh.

"Hey, Jillian, I want to ask you something important," Stephanie said, changing the subject for the moment. "And I think right here in front of my very best friends is the best place to do it."

She seemed so serious, and Jillian wasn't sure what was about to come her way, especially when the rest of the group had grown so quiet. "Sure. What's up?"

"Remember when I told you a few weeks ago that I was contracted for a huge job to decorate and design some fantasy suites for a privately owned hotel?"

Jillian nodded. She'd been thrilled to hear the news, and very happy for Stephanie who'd helped Jillian create a sultry, romantic playroom for her and Dean to enjoy. The woman had an eye for interior design, and coupling that with sexier, more dramatic elements made for some very erotic concepts that had garnered her awards along with a very exclusive, wealthy clientele. Just recently one of her fantasy bedrooms had been featured in Romantic Homes Magazine, which had increased her exposure.

"Well, I've been doing everything myself for years, trying to get to the point where the business is financially secure and I've made a name for Fantasy Bedrooms, and I'm finally there," Stephanie went on, her tone both excited and a bit nervous. "I'm at the point where I need help with the designing, especially now with the hotel contract I just signed, and I want someone I trust and who knows and understands my esthetic."

"I'm really sorry, but I don't know anyone who has interior design experience," Jillian said, feeling bad that she wasn't able to offer better resources.

Stephanie gave her a lop-sided smile, her eyes glimmering with humor. "That's good, because I want to hire *you* as my assistant designer. If you're interested."

"Me?" She stared at the other woman in shock, certain she misunderstood. "Are you serious? I don't have any interior design experience."

"Sometimes, it's not about experience," Stephanie shrugged. "Sometimes it's purely gut instinct and the ability to bring a creative vision to life."

Jillian shook her head, still not convinced. "What makes you think I have that kind of ability?"

"I've seen your gorgeous, custom-built home, which you decorated all on your own," Stephanie said, clearly having thought this through. "And you did an amazing job on the playroom. I really was just a consultant who helped with a few things. The design and color scheme was all your idea."

"Oh, wow." Jillian's heart was pounding crazily in her chest, an adrenaline rush of excitement she couldn't deny. Stephanie was offering her the chance to be a part of something big and meaningful, something she'd thoroughly enjoy that would get her out of the house and provide her with that daily stimulation she desperately craved.

She couldn't believe this opportunity had come her way at just the right time, and she was floored, and flattered, that Stephanie had that kind of faith in her. She really wanted to try this, to test the waters . . . she *needed* this.

The only obstacle standing in her way was convincing Dean. Easier said than done, she knew, and hated the twist of anxiety knotting in her stomach. She never thought of herself as the type of woman who needed her husband's approval to do anything, but ultimately she wanted his blessing and support, and she honestly wasn't sure if it would happen. She didn't want to hurt him, but she desperately needed this creative outlet for herself.

"You do know that we're all waiting anxiously for you to answer and say *yes*, so we can celebrate with another drink, right?" Raina said, giving her a well-meaning nudge.

Jillian glanced around the room, at all the women she now called friends. When she'd told Dean about joining the girls for their get-together, he'd been indulgent. Had even encouraged her to go out and have fun. But accepting a job offer . . . that was something else entirely, because she knew the emotional issues that came with her husband coming to terms with his wife *working*. He viewed himself as the male, the provider and protector, everything his father had never been, and she understood her husband well enough to know that he'd equate her need for more as a failure on his part.

She and Dean had never had a real issue or bone of contention in their marriage, a conflict that would cause a huge argument or fight. Jillian knew with every fiber of her being that telling her husband she was going to work outside of the house would be the impetus for their first major battle of wills.

But even with that knowledge, she wasn't about to back down from the one thing she'd ever wanted just for herself . . . even if that meant forcing her husband to face some of his deepest fears.

"Yes, I would love to be your assistant designer," Jillian said, wishing she could commit one hundred percent to Stephanie's offer and celebrate the exciting changes to come. "But I do need to talk to Dean first."

Stephanie grinned. "Do whatever it takes to persuade your husband, because I desperately need you."

"Blow jobs are the best way to get a man to say yes to anything," Raina said, as if she'd had experience in the matter. "We're counting on you to make it happen, Jillian."

She laughed and assured them that she'd do her part, but she was already dreading the conversation, and the argument, to come.

JILLIAN PACED ANXIOUSLY in her bedroom, trying to gather the fortitude to walk into Dean's office down the hall where he was finishing up details on an important client presentation, and tell him about her job offer.

The timing certainly wasn't ideal. Then again, when it came to Dean, there would never be a good time to discuss her desire to go to work for Stephanie. But with him leaving in the morning for a week long business trip to New York, she needed to broach the subject with him so she could get back to Stephanie with a firm answer.

Exhaling a deep breath and shaking off her nerves, she headed determinedly to his office and knocked on the open door. As soon as he glanced up from the paperwork spread out on his desk, she spoke. "I know you're busy, but can I have a few minutes to talk to you?"

"Sure," he said, just as she knew he would, though his brows furrowed in concern as he watched her walk into the room. "Everything okay?"

"Everything is fine," she assured him, and sat down in one of the leather club chairs in front of his desk. Her husband was a man who appreciated a direct approach, so she didn't waste time trying to couch her words. "Stephanie, the woman who helped me design and decorate the playroom, offered me a job as her assistant designer."

"Oh." He leaned back in his chair, the flicker of surprise she initially saw in his gaze quickly replaced by a schooled expression that masked his emotions. "That was nice of her."

She heard the placating note to his voice, and didn't miss the way he deliberately avoided the crux of her statement, *that she'd been offered a job*. She hadn't interrupted him to make small talk, and her very sharp and intelligent husband knew it, too. He was playing it cool and not jumping to any conclusions. Either that or he was mentally preparing an argument as to why she didn't *need* to work.

She suspected the latter.

"I'd like to accept her offer," she said point-blank, so there was no misconstruing what this conversation was about.

"Why?" His brusque tone was underscored with a hint of agitation. "You don't need to work, and we don't need the money."

She nearly rolled her eyes at his predictable response, but caught herself. "This isn't about *needing* to work, or money. It's about doing something more with my life now that the boys are grown and gone and I don't have to take care of them any longer. Quite honestly, I'm bored being at home all day with nothing to do."

His jaw clenched. "Are you unhappy?"

Of course his mind would go there first, because up to this point in their marriage she'd been perfectly content being a stay at home wife and mother. And she hated that he'd equate her need to work with being dissatisfied emotionally, or with him.

"This decision has nothing to do with you, or being unhappy in our marriage, which I'm *not*," she said, her words gentle, but her tone remained firm. "You have Noble and Associates, and I'd like to get out of the house during the day, be around people, and do something productive with my time that stimulates me creatively. And this job as Stephanie's assistant would give me exactly that."

His entire body had grown stiff, his demeanor tense. "I don't want you to work." His reply was succinct and blunt.

"Why not?" She'd never pushed her husband so hard on an issue, but this opportunity was important to her and she wasn't backing down or giving up.

His gaze darkened to a stormy shade of gray. "You know exactly *why*, Jillian," he said, an unmistakable thread of anger vibrating in his voice.

Yes, she knew precisely *why* he was so adverse to the idea of her working and she wasn't going to make him say the reasons out loud. She'd definitely provoked him and stirred up childhood angst and all those resentments toward his own deadbeat, insolent father.

They both knew *why* he felt the strong need to provide financially for his family, to be the kind of father and reliable, dependable, husband his dad had never been. Dean harbored a ton of guilt over his mother's suicide and blamed himself for not being able to save her from his abusive father and a life of drudgery, and those emotions had driven him to be a better man than his father in every way, and he'd succeeded beyond what most people strive for.

Yet despite what Dean had made of his life and how he'd made his family a priority, those painful memories made it difficult for him let go of the provider/protector mentality he'd embraced their entire marriage.

"I'm not your mother," she softly, knowing she was treading into very dangerous, emotional territory, but it had to be done. "You've always taken care of me, and I know you always will. You've given me and the boys a great life, and I've loved being able to stay home for them, and you, the past twenty years. But I'm at a point in my life when I want, no *need*, to take this job."

He immediately shut down, his withdrawal from her, and the conversation, nearly palpable. "Look, I've got a ton of things to get done tonight, including this presentation for Corporate Crises Management, before I leave for New York in the morning. If I don't have a presentation for the client, we don't get the contract. We'll talk about it when I get back home."

He was brushing her off, and she couldn't deny that his disregard hurt. A lot. "So, what I want or need isn't a priority right now?"

He sighed heavily, wearily even, as he rubbed his forehead with his fingers. "I didn't say that. I just don't have time tonight to have this argument."

An argument he clearly intended to win.

Well, so did she. Which meant they were at a stalemate.

He glanced back down at the paperwork on his desk, a quiet dismissal, and Jillian couldn't stem the disappointment and frustration coursing through her. They'd come so far in the past few months, emotionally and physically. They'd opened up to one another in ways they never had before, they'd built a fortress of trust she'd believed would carry over into other aspects of their marriage, and this felt like a huge slide backwards.

She stood up and walked to the door, then stopped and turned back around. He didn't look up at her, but she knew he could hear her, and that's all that mattered. "I'd really like to have your blessing to do this, but just so the two of us are clear, I don't *need* your approval to accept the job, Dean. If you don't learn to compromise and trust *me*, it's going to cause resentment and anger to build between us."

It was a harsh statement to a man who liked to be in control of everything, but she didn't want her husband to think or believe that she'd just roll over and accept his dictate. He might not want her to work, but she'd made her decision and it was up to him to come to terms with this new shift in their marriage.

CHAPTER 6

"Are you done working for the night?"

Jillian's soft voice drifted though Dean's cellphone, making his chest ache as it did every evening when he called home to check in with her. He'd been in New York for the longest, most miserable week of his life, and he missed her. Not just the physical component of being together, but their easy conversations, their flirtatious banter, and her laughter . . . all of that had been sorely lacking since the night she'd walked into his office and turned his perfectly well-ordered life, and everything in it, upside down.

He felt as though the earth had shifted beneath him with her announcement, shaking the very foundation of their relationship in ways he never saw coming. And this newly determined, independent side to Jillian honestly scared the shit out of him.

"Yes, I'm done for the night," he replied as he ran his finger along the rim of his glass of Scotch, contemplating the idea of just getting fucking drunk so he didn't have to think about all the doubts and uncertainties eating away at him. "The presentation was approved and the contract signed today. I'll be heading back home in the morning."

"That's great news about the contract," she said, much too pleasantly, as if he was talking to a stranger rather his wife of twenty years. "Where are you now?"

God, he hated the small talk and the too-polite tone of her voice. But he'd caused this awful tension between them with his negative reaction and his refusal to discuss the job offer with her, and by avoiding the conversation every single night when they talked on the phone. But when he thought about the changes she wanted to make to their marriage, changes that made his stomach churn for various reasons, he just couldn't bring himself to go there, mentally or emotionally.

He downed the rest of his drink, relishing the burn of liquor down his throat, and answered her. "I just had dinner, and I'm having a drink in the hotel bar before heading up to my room for the evening."

"I'm glad everything went well with the presentation and client," she said, yet another amicable reply that hit Dean like a direct punch in the gut.

A strained silence stretched between them, until she finally said, "I guess I'll see you tomorrow afternoon when you get home. Travel safe and I love you."

"I love you, too," he said, and felt his heart tighten in his chest as the line disconnected, making him all too aware of the emotional and physical distance separating them.

He set his phone on the polished mahogany bar and scrubbed a hand along his jaw. Yep, he was going to get shit-faced drunk so he didn't have to think about the damage he was doing to his marriage, all because he had deep-seated issues with his wife wanting to *work*.

He motioned to the bartender for another order of Scotch, realizing that he'd normally be pumped up after cinching such a huge contract with a new client and celebrating the coup, but instead he was about to drown his sorrows in premium liquor, along with his growing fears.

It wasn't easy for him to admit, but Jillian's parting remark to him a week ago and the underlying ultimatum in her words made him feel completely helpless over the situation, and he absolutely *hated* that loss of control. For him, his wife was disrupting the predictable, stable *status quo* of their marriage, and asserting herself in ways she never had before.

And that's what scared him the most . . . her newfound independence and fortitude. It had all started a few months ago, when she'd walked into his office to seduce him. That hot sexual confidence of hers was intoxicating in the bedroom and playroom, but he'd never anticipated that those changes in her would integrate into all aspects of their relationship. That she'd become more determined and unwavering in her convictions.

The bartender placed a fresh glass of Macallan in front of him, cleared off the empty one, and headed down to the opposite side of the bar to help another customer, leaving Dean with his turbulent thoughts once again and forcing him to face the realization of just how selfish he was being about his wife's need to spread her wings and pursue something that would make her happy. Especially when she'd done so much for *him*.

She'd raised their young sons alone while he'd been in the military and training for the SEALS, had run the household smoothly and efficiently over the years, and had been a supportive wife while he'd spent unending hours building his business, never once complaining or nagging him about all the late nights at the office, or all the time he spent away from home. She'd fulfilled all his needs, had giving *him* the stability that he'd always craved as a result of his shitty childhood—not the other way around.

The realization of how one-sided and self-centered he'd been was like a sharp slap in the face and a much needed wake-up call. All week long he'd told himself not wanting Jillian to work was all about taking care of her like a husband should, but when he dug deeper at the truth of the matter, he exposed the part of himself that was afraid that once she focused on a new and exciting career, she wouldn't need *him* any longer.

And how fucking pathetic was that, he thought, as he swallowed a mouthful of scotch.

There was no doubt in Dean's mind that if he denied Jillian, he'd only succeed in pushing her away, and driving a deeper wedge of resentment between them, and she'd accept the job, anyway. Ultimately, he wasn't willing to risk losing her, or permanently damaging the key element of trust in their marriage, and that meant shoving aside his own insecurities and stepping up to the plate to support his wife's desires. He needed to let her chase her own dreams, and come home to him happy and fulfilled. He owed her that. She *deserved* that freedom and joy—guilt free, even if it was one of the most difficult things he'd ever had to do.

Swallowing his own stupid pride, he picked up his cellphone to call Jillian back, and grovel if necessary. But before he could tap in his passcode to unlock the main screen, he felt someone slide onto the empty barstool beside him, followed by a low, sultry voice asking, "Care to buy a girl a drink?"

Knowing the person was talking to him, he absently glanced her way to gently turn her down, and did a quick double-take at the woman who'd claimed the seat and was turned toward him. Bright emerald green eyes, fringed by ridiculously thick lashes, stared at him expectantly as she waited for him to respond. Platinum blonde, chin length hair with wispy bangs framed her pretty face, and full lips, painted a bright cherry red—his favorite color—smiled at him.

Shocked and speechless, he couldn't stop his curious gaze from traveling lower, taking in her lipstick red halter-style top that molded to her breasts and provided an eye-catching amount of cleavage. The straps tied together at the nape of her neck, leaving her back completely bare—indicating she wasn't wearing a bra. The hem of her tight black leather mini-skirt ended mid-thigh, giving him a glimpse of smooth, silky-looking skin he was tempted to touch.

Heated awareness thrummed through him and settled in his groin, and he had to admit it took extreme effort to drag his gaze back up to her face, like a gentleman. But even then, those crimson lips prompted some pretty illicit fantasies that had no business popping into his head. Of that sweet red mouth opening, and that plump bottom lip providing a perfect resting place for his hardening dick.

Laughter and amusement glimmered in

her eyes. "What's the matter? Cat got your tongue?"

He cleared his throat, still trying to process . . . *her*. "I, uh, just wasn't expecting company."

"*Company* is an interesting choice of word," she murmured, the seductive tone of her voice stroking down his spine like a lover's caress. "Are you looking for *company* tonight?"

There was no mistaking her meaning, and despite the devil on his shoulder prodding him to say *yes*, he quickly shook his head, and swirled the last of the amber liquid in his glass "Uh, no, not really. I was just having a drink before I head up to my room for the night."

She blinked those long lashes at him, and arched a delicate brow. "Alone?"

"Yes, alone," he said, not sounding nearly as firm as he should have.

"Maybe I could convince you to change your mind about that." She leaned closer, deliberately placed a hand on his thigh, and squeezed suggestively. "After all, providing *company* is my business."

The corner of his mouth quirked upward. "So, you're a prostitute?"

She laughed, unoffended. "I prefer the term call girl. It's more discreet and respectable." She continued stroking his leg, the tips of her fingers coming much too close to the erection growing in his slacks as a result of her touch. "And just to put it out there so you don't have to ask, my rates are quite reasonable, depending on what you're interested in."

The sexual invitation in her voice beckoned to the most basic male part of him, and with effort he lifted his left hand to show her the gold band encircling his finger. "Sorry, but I'm married."

"I won't tell if you don't." She gave him a deliciously naughty smile. "As a working girl, I subscribe to the motto that what happens in this hotel, stays in this hotel."

He laughed, and had to give her credit for being so persistent. He knew this distraction was only temporary before reality intruded, but he latched onto it and played along, curious to see where this encounter would lead. "What's your name?"

"Candy," she said, the name teeming with innuendo, as she slowly trailed her fingers down her chest toward her ample cleavage. "Because I'm as sweet as sugar . . . everywhere. These, especially, taste like hard cherry candies."

Jesus. His gaze lowered to the thin material covering her breasts and the puckered nipples she was referring to. His mouth watered in anticipation, and he swallowed hard and reined in the lust burning through his veins. "Okay, *Candy*," he said, his voice much too gravelly as he signaled the bartender back down to his end of the counter, who arrived within a few short seconds. "Tell the man what you'd like to drink."

She thought for a moment then said very cheekily, "Can you give me a Screaming Orgasm, please?"

The other man's gaze took in her glossy red lips then shifted to the straining nipples that were damn hard to miss and grinned wolfishly. "It would be my pleasure to give you a screaming orgasm." He set a shot glass on the counter and reached for a bottle of vodka.

"Thank you," she replied in sexy, flirtatious tone as she slanted a sly look Dean's way. "It's been a while and I might need more than one."

The guy chuckled, clearly enjoying the sexy banter between them as he added Bailey's and Kahlua to the mix. "I'm all about pleasing the customer," he teased with a wink as he set the drink on a napkin in front of her. "If you require multiple screaming orgasms, I'm your man."

Feeling much too possessive over *Candy*, Dean found himself glaring at the other man, who backed off as soon as he saw his darkening expression.

"You scared the poor man off," she said, amusement lacing her voice as her jeweled green eyes met his. "At least *someone* is willing to accommodate my needs tonight."

He wisely kept quiet and finished off his Macallan, adding the last of the liquor to the confusion swirling inside of him, then pushed the empty glass aside.

"So, you're in a hotel bar, so I'm

assuming you're from out of town?" she asked conversationally.

"Yes," he replied automatically. "I'm here on business."

She dipped a finger into her creamy drink and lazily stirred the contents with the digit. "Business men are my favorite kind of clients," she said, back into character of call girl once again.

"Really?" he drawled, intrigued despite himself. "And why is that?"

"Because they're usually the kinkiest," she revealed as she locked her gaze on his and sucked her finger into her mouth, slowly licking off the creamy concoction in a way that was incredibly phallic. "And I'm willing to do all those dirty, depraved things that their wives won't."

Ah, fuck. "What's your specialty?" He was dying to know.

She gave him a secretive smile. "I've been told that I'm amazing at sucking cock, but I'm open to trying *anything*. The kinkier, the better." She lifted the shot glass to her mouth and downed the screaming orgasm in one easy swallow, then swiped the remnants of cream from her bottom lip with a lick of her tongue. "Let's go up to your room and I'll show you how down and dirty things can get."

He was so fucking turned on he could barely think straight. "I'll take you to my room, but no kissing, touching, or actual fucking. That's for my wife, only." *Jesus, was he really negotiating with her?*

"That's a shame and doesn't leave a whole lot left to do," she said, clearly disappointed in his "no physical contact" decree. She tipped her head, the ends of her platinum blonde bob sliding along her jaw as she studied him for a moment, sizing him up. "You look like the kind of man who likes to be in charge and give orders. How about you just tell me what to do and sit back and watch the show?"

The temptation was just too great for him to resist and promised to take his mind off of all the issues he'd left unresolved with Jillian in San Diego. He was thousands of miles away from home, and if *Candy* wanted to be his entertainment for the night, he was more than willing to oblige.

"Let's go," he said, and abruptly stood before he changed his mind and put an end to this game she was playing.

He tossed two twenties onto the counter to cover the tab, then headed out of the hotel bar with her following behind so he didn't violate his own *no touching* rule. Inside the elevator, he swiped his keycard and pressed the button for the penthouse floor.

She leaned against the opposite wall of where he was standing, and it didn't matter where he looked because the mirrors lining the cubicle reflected her *everywhere*, imprinting her on his brain whether he wanted her to be there or not, and reminding him just how erotic mirrors could be during foreplay and sex.

He met her seductive gaze from across the elevator, his body instinctively responding to the way her eyes brazenly ate him up. And *Jesus Christ*, the way she stared at the thick length of his shaft straining the fabric of his slacks and hungrily licked her lips nearly destroyed his resolve to keep this a hands-off encounter. It was all he could do to restrain himself from closing the distance between them and kissing her, touching her, and fucking her every way imaginable.

A soft ping announced their arrival, and the elevator doors quietly opened, saving him from doing anything stupid. She walked out ahead of him directly into the penthouse suite, providing him with another form of torture of watching the confident sway of her hips and taking in her perfectly rounded ass beneath the tight black leather mini-skirt.

"Nice place," she commented as she looked around the spacious living area with an adjoining kitchen and dining room with a table that easily seated ten. She moved toward the floor to ceiling windows that overlooked New York City lit up at night. "The view from up here is amazing."

Bringing her up to his place wasn't about pleasantries and the kind of polite conversation he'd been forced to endure the past week with his wife. No, he had something far more dirty and daring in mind for Candy.

"The bedroom is in here," he said, and walked into the huge master suite. A few seconds later she strolled inside, and before she could say a word, he took complete control of the situation. "Leave your clothes and heels on and lay down in the middle of the bed," he ordered.

Her green eyes widened slightly at the brusque command. Then she shrugged, placed her small purse on the night stand, and climbed up onto the huge king-sized mattress to do as he instructed. "Whatever you want. You're the paying customer."

"Yes, I am," he said gruffly, liking the power that gave him. "Pull your skirt up to your waist."

Her fingers grabbed the hem of the skirt and she shimmied the tight leather up over her hips, a naughty girl smirk curving her red lips as she displayed her smooth, bare mound and revealed the fact that she wasn't wearing any underwear.

Fuck. His stomach muscles clenched with a primal need to claim, and he had to forcibly tamp down the urge. Oh, he was *so* going to make her pay for that indiscretion, walking around New York City without any panties on.

Her knees were pressed much too primly together, and he walked to the foot of the bed and stared up at her, his blood already running like molten lava through his veins. "Spread your legs wide so I can see everything."

Unabashedly, she parted her thighs and planted her stilettos three feet apart on the mattress, exposing every inch of her glistening, gorgeous sex. "Touch yourself." His voice vibrated with the low, rough command.

Her hand moved down between her legs, her fingers sliding leisurely through the damp folds and dipping into her core. Slick moisture gathered on the tips of her fingers, and she brought them up to her clitoris, stroking that hard knot of flesh with slow precise strokes that made her back arch off the bed. Her lashes fluttered closed, her hips began undulating, and her red lips parted with a soft, pleasurable gasp that make his dick pound and ache.

He was burning up with lust, his skin so

hot the waves of heat suffused his entire body. Yanking his shirt off, he tossed it aside, but left his pants on, even though his cock was demanding to be let free. He continued to watch Candy get herself off, and knew by the rapid rise and fall of her chest that she was close to coming.

Not ready to allow her that relief just yet, he grabbed both of her ankles and flipped her onto her stomach, then dragged her all the way down to where he was standing at the foot of the bed. A startled sound escaped her, but she didn't protest when he took hold of her hips and pulled her ass up into the air so that she was on her knees, her legs still spread, with her upper body pressed against the mattress.

With her skirt rucked up around her hips, the position was lewd and raunchy and exactly what he wanted. "Keep touching yourself," he growled, enjoying the control he had over her, and the situation.

Her hand returned to do his bidding, giving him a close up view of her drenched pussy and burgeoning clit. His nostrils flared as he inhaled the heady, aroused scent of her and watched those slender, well-manicured fingers slip, slide and stoke, until being an idle spectator was no longer enough. Figuring he'd already crossed a few lines tonight, he reached out and dragged a finger along her wet slit and spread that sweet cream along the crevice of her bottom.

She gasped in shock and her head whipped around to stare at him over her shoulder. Amusement shimmered in her dark, sultry gaze, and her lips eased up in a too provocative smile. "I thought you said no touching."

He smirked right back at her. "I fucking changed my mind." To prove his point, he pushed two long fingers into her weeping channel and smacked her ass with his free hand.

Another sharp gasp filled the air between them, followed by a low moan of pleasure when he caressed the warm splotch of color appearing on her smooth, pale bottom. "Rough play is going to cost you extra."

"Then add it to my tab, because I plan to get my money's worth," he replied as he thrust his fingers deep inside her once more and spanked her other cheek. "I want to hear you scream your orgasm, Candy."

She laid her head back down on the bed and closed her eyes, her fingers circling her clit, while her hips rocked back and forth on the long, thick fingers pumping in and out of her body, penetrating a bit deeper each time. He added another stinging slap to her tender backside and she started to pant. Two more swats to her rosy-hued flesh and her free hand clutched at the covers for leverage as her sex clamped and contracted around his fingers as her climaxed peaked.

And then she *screamed*, long and loud, until her voice turned hoarse and her body went lax, and *Jesus Christ*, he nearly came in his pants just because watching her was so fucking sexy and erotic.

With a soft, sated sigh, she rolled to her back in the middle of the bed, her slender legs still splayed so he could see her pink, swollen and oh-so-inviting pussy. Her half-lidded gaze lowered to the monstrous erection still confined in his slacks, and she reached up and untied the halter straps from behind her neck, then lowered the two panels of fabric to her waist, exposing her full breasts and the enticing, hardened beads of her nipples to his avid gaze.

Biting her lower lip, she took her breasts in her hands and squeezed them together, clearly tempting him by her brazen, seductive display. "Don't you want me?" she asked huskily.

He took in the chin-length blonde hair, the unfamiliar green eyes, and red stained lips that was all *wrong*, despite the fact that his body felt otherwise. "I want my wife," he said, unable to ignore the truth of that statement.

The look in her eyes softened at his words, but she didn't stop her attempts to sway him. "Well, she's not here and surely there's something you've fantasized about doing to her, but you thought maybe she'd be too shocked to agree?"

"Lately, she's been pretty adventurous and daring," he said, the corner of his mouth quirking up in a grin as he watched her play with her breasts. "But yeah, there is one thing I've thought about . . ."

"Here's your chance to do it," she said, a challenging gleam in her eyes.

In a flash, he was on the bed and kneeling astride her stomach, quickly working the button and zipper on his pants to free his cock before he changed his mind about what he was about to reveal. "I want to fuck your tits."

Her mouth dropped open, then snapped shut again, though her eyes remained wide and startled by his very kinky request.

He chuckled, the sound low and deep and completely depraved as he shoved his pants down to his hips, released his shaft, and began stroking the hard, hot length in his palm while she watched. "What? Is that too *shocking* for you, Candy?"

She quickly recovered and lifted her chin in a show of confidence. "Of course not. In fact, there's lubrication in my purse if you need it. I always come prepared, for *anything*."

He raised a brow at her sassy reply, but

said nothing as he reached over to the night stand, opened her small purse, and retrieved the lube that no *working girl* would ever leave home without. He squirted a line of the slippery substance between her breasts and smeared it around until he was assured a smooth, slick ride.

"Press your tits tight together so I can fuck them," he ordered gruffly, unable to deny the excitement spiking through him as she immediately obeyed. Taking his cock in hand, he inserted the engorged head between her plumped up breasts and pushed his hips forward, sliding into . . . *heaven*.

He groaned and shuddered as he pulled back, then surged in again. *"Holy hell,"* he uttered on a breath, his eyes closing for a moment as he tried to process just how good it felt to have his dick cocooned in such softness and warmth.

"Don't stop now," she teased, rubbing her breasts together so that she created another layer of sensation along his enveloped cock.

He opened his eyes, met her beguiling

gaze, and gave into the need pounding through him. Leaning over her for a better thrusting angle, he grabbed onto the headboard and began to piston his hips—slowly at first, then gradually picking up the pace until he'd created a heated friction that short circuited his brain.

Forcing himself to hold back, he looked down, so incredibly turned on by the erotic sight of his cock burrowing between her lush cleavage and equally satisfied by just how aroused this scenario was making her, too. Her face was flushed, and she arched her back to accommodate his steady thrusts, keeping her breasts squeezed tight together. She pinched her elongated nipples, moaned oh-so-softly, and he lost it completely.

He growled deep in his throat as his orgasm slammed into him and he came hot and hard, his rigid cock pulsing, throbbing, while his essence splashed across her chest and throat in hot, sticky torrent.

By the time the last shock waves died away, he was gasping for breath. He sat back on her stomach, trying to recover from the mind-blowing experience.

"Was it good?" she asked, her tone deliciously smug.

"You know it was." Unable to stop himself, he reached out and trailed a finger through the milky drops of semen on her skin. "Do you know what it's called when a man comes on a woman's chest and throat?"

She arched a curious brow. "No, what?"

He gave her a wicked smile. "A pearl necklace." He dragged that same finger, now slick with his release, along her bottom lip, then boldly pushed it into her mouth.

"Umm." Meeting his gaze, she swirled her tongue around his finger, brazenly licking and sucking away the taste of him. "I love pearls," she said huskily, once he withdrew his finger from her warm, wet mouth.

"My wife is very fond of them, as well."

As soon as the intimate words were out, as soon as those green eyes staring up at him softened with emotion, a wealth of guilt crashed over him, jolting him right out of the fantasy. Reality rudely intruded, and those same insecurities that had driven him to shut out his wife the night before he'd left town suddenly overwhelmed him all over again. His chest tightened, and needing distance to regain his composure, he moved off her and headed into the adjoining bathroom, closing the door behind him.

He turned on the shower, and as steam began to fill the spacious area he stripped off the rest of his clothes, then stepped beneath the hot spray, letting the water drench his hair and sluice down his body. A moment later, the door opened and through the clear glass cubicle he watched Jillian tentatively walk inside the bathroom.

She'd stripped away every trace of *Candy*. The blonde wig was gone, allowing her beautiful, dark brown hair to tumble freely around her shoulders. She'd removed those green contacts, wiped away the red lipstick, and taken off her sexy *call girl* clothes. She was as naked as he was, and as she quietly stepped into the shower with him and lifted her gaze to his, the renewed fortitude in her sky blue eyes twisted his stomach into a gigantic knot of uncertainty.

After a week of small talk on the phone that skirted the underlying issue between them, why had she shown up now? The question bounced around in his head, dredging up answers that played into his deepest, most basic fears. What if she'd flown all the way to New York for one last fun sexcapade before asking for a divorce so she could do whatever the hell she wanted without ever having to ask him? What if she'd decided that she liked being independent and didn't need him anymore?

His hands clenched into fists at his sides, and he knew his expression reflected the anguish and unease swirling inside of him. He'd always done an impeccable job of suppressing those too-vulnerable weaknesses from his wife, but when he was faced with the very real possibility of losing her, he found it impossible to conceal his emotional turmoil.

She saw it, too. Her gaze softened and

she closed the distance between them so she was only inches away, the spray from the shower getting her wet, too. "Dean, we need to talk," she said, her words gentle, yet undeniably determined.

Not ready to face the inevitable, he did the one thing he knew would stall the discussion to come, *coward that he was*. Reaching out, he threaded his fingers through her damp hair, tipped her head back, and crushed his mouth to hers. Her lips parted on a gasp of surprise, and he took full advantage, thrusting his tongue deep inside while backing her up against the cool tiled wall and pressing their bodies tight together.

Much to his relief, she wrapped her arms around his neck and kissed him back, her mouth giving and taking with equal measure. He couldn't get enough of her, his need and hunger so great it threatened to engulf him and leave him drowning.

He pulled his mouth from hers and buried his face against the sweet curve of her neck as the shower spray pummeled his back. He was panting for breath, his aching, throbbing cock pressing insistently against her soft stomach. "Jillian . . ." He groaned her name, uncaring of how desperate his voice had become. "I need to be inside of you. I need to be a part of you. *Please.*" It wasn't a demand, but a request, one he needed her to acknowledge and accept on her own terms.

"Yes," she whispered.

As soon as the word was out of her mouth he pulled her out of the shower, leaving the water running in his haste, and had her flat on her back on the bed within thirty seconds. His slick, wet body moved over hers, and she automatically spread her legs for him, allowing him to slide inside of her, all the way to the hilt, in one smooth, driving thrust. She wrapped her legs around his waist and arched beneath him, the scrape of her nails across his back urging him to move.

He wanted to go slow. Wanted to make this last. Wanted to make love to her and be soft and tender and romantic. But she knew what he needed the most, knew his mind and body and what was in the deepest recesses of his soul. No matter the issues between the two of them, no matter the power struggle *outside* of the bedroom, here, beneath him, she was willing to submit to his every desire, and that knowledge slayed and humbled him.

"Take me harder, Dean," she said huskily as her hands skimmed down the slope of his back to clutch his ass in an attempt increase the pace of his thrusts. "Take me *deeper*."

Ahh, fuck. She knew exactly how to appeal to his darker, more dominant side, knew exactly what to do to engage him and he was helpless to resist her efforts. Grasping her wrists, he stretched her arms above her head and restrained her hands by linking their fingers together, providing him with the ultimate control he craved, and allowing him complete and primitive possession of her body and pleasure.

He flexed his hips, tunneling into her faster, forging deeper with every demanding, ruthless stroke and fucking her like a force of nature. With a helpless, unraveling moan, her head rolled back, her eyes closed, and he felt those internal contractions begin to flutter around his cock, milking his shaft with an incredible liquid warmth.

"Look at me," he ordered gruffly, needing that connection with her.

With effort, Jillian's eyes opened once again, the heat and adoration in the depths of her gaze his final undoing. Her fingers tightened around his as if she needed the anchor as she tumbled over the edge of her orgasm and came apart for him with a soft cry of pleasure, while he continued to pound into her until his own searing release scorched through him, leaving him spent, wasted, and his emotions scraped raw.

He moved off her, and with a content sigh she snuggled against his chest, soft, warm, and sated. And that's how he planned to keep her, all night long, because come the morning there would be no avoiding the conversation she'd come all the way to New York to have with him.

CHAPTER 7

Jillian woke up alone in the big, king-sized bed she'd shared with her husband last night, not surprised, but definitely disappointed, to find him gone. She reached out and touched the pillow beside hers, hating that Dean found it necessary to put distance between them this morning when they'd shared so much physically and emotionally the evening before.

There hadn't been much of an opportunity to talk during the course of the night, not when Dean had made it a point to keep her hands and mouth *very* busy whenever he thought she was going to broach the subject of her working. And because he was a master at knowing exactly what turned her on, his stall tactics had worked much too well.

She exhaled a frustrated stream of breath. How long did he intend to evade the huge disagreement still hanging over them like a dark cloud? It didn't matter, because she had every intention of confronting Dean and getting it all out into the open. He couldn't avoid her forever, and wherever he'd disappeared to, he'd eventually have to return. As far as she was concerned, they weren't leaving New York until they'd resolved their issues and they came to an understanding.

With a shake of her head, she got up and padded into the bathroom and used the facilities. Realizing she only had last night's clothes with her, she slipped into the plush white robe hanging from a hook on the back of the door, secured the sash, then combed the tangles from her hair and brushed her teeth. She'd left her luggage with the concierge when she'd arrived at the hotel yesterday afternoon, and she needed to call the front desk to have it delivered so she'd have something to wear for the day other than the skimpy outfit she'd worn to seduce her husband down in the bar.

The thought of how thoroughly she'd surprised Dean made her smile.

The entire week without Dean had been long and miserable. She always missed him when he was away on a business trip, but their evening phone conversations had always been warm, fun, and sometimes very sexy. This time, they'd been cool, polite, and abrupt, and with each day that passed she could feel that chasm deepening between them, until she feared they might not be able to get past the conflict that had put them at a mutual stand-off.

Then, two days ago, she'd been down in their playroom, thinking of how far they'd come in just a few months, how much closer they'd grown emotionally and physically, all because she'd been open and honest about wanting to heat up their sex lives, and Dean allowing himself to embrace those darker impulses he'd suppressed for way too long.

On a whim, she'd reached into the decorative crystal vase she'd bought for them to use as a place where they could write down and share their secret, provocative fantasies, to use whenever they needed inspiration, and withdrew a folded piece of paper. When she read Dean's bold handwriting and the sexy scenario he'd divulged —*being seduced by a call girl at a bar*—she took it as a sign of fate of what she needed to do to break the ice between them and hopefully put things back on track again.

Last night's seduction had been a huge success, but unfortunately they were no closer to a resolution than when he'd left for his business trip a week ago.

Figuring she'd camp out in the suite until he returned from wherever he'd gone, she opened the master bedroom door and headed into the adjoining living room. She came to an abrupt stop when she saw Dean sitting at the dining table, going through messages on his phone while eating a plate filled with eggs, bacon, and hash browns.

Freshly showered and shaved, and wearing a tan t-shirt and jeans, he looked breath-takingly gorgeous. "You're here," she said, blinking a few times to make sure he wasn't a figment of her imagination.

His light gray eyes met hers, a hint of wariness flickering in the depths, the only indication that he was feeling slightly cautious about what the morning would bring. "You sound shocked."

"I guess I am," she admitted honestly as she walked toward the table, and him. "You weren't in bed, so I just assumed you were gone."

He shut off his phone and set it aside. "I've been here all morning, waiting for you to wake up so we can . . . talk."

His tone was reluctant, but she gave him credit for taking the initiative. It gave her hope that was he more open to listening and understanding *her* needs in this marriage.

"I ordered up a few things for your breakfast," he said, waving a hand toward the nearby room service cart.

"Thanks." She poured coffee from a

carafe, added cream and sugar, and smiled when she saw that he'd ordered her favorite breakfast staples: yogurt, granola, and mixed fruit. She set everything on the table, and sat down next to him.

"I can't believe you flew all the way to New York to fulfill one of my fantasies," he said, a hint of a smile touching the corner of his mouth right before he took a drink of his coffee.

"I know it was an extreme thing to do," she said, mixing her yogurt and granola together. "But I didn't want you to come home angry, and it just seemed like a good way to dissipate some of that tension between us and help us get back on track."

He raised a dark, sable brow. "So, you think I can be mollified with hot sex?"

"You're a *man*, aren't you?" His smirk was all she needed to know that she'd made her point, so she continued. "My thought was, when we walk back into that house, I want us to be united in our marriage *and* my desire to work. The two go hand in hand, and we're not leaving here until that happens."

He frowned at her. "What is that supposed to mean?"

She swallowed a bite of sweet cantaloupe, preparing for battle. "It means, I expect you to compromise with me, so that *when* I go to work there aren't any resentments between us."

He slowly, silently, laid his fork down on his nearly empty plate. "So, you've already decided to take the job?"

"I have." She lifted her chin determinedly. "I start on Wednesday."

He exhaled a deep breath and said, "Okay."

She stared at him, momentarily confused. She'd been expecting an argument, not such an easy acquiescence from her very stubborn husband. "Are you really okay, or are you just saying that to appease me?" Because that wasn't good enough for her and resolved nothing. "Please, tell me what's going on in your head."

He was quiet for so long, she thought he wasn't going to answer. And then he did.

"There's a lot going on in my head," he

finally said. "So much, that I'm not sure where to start."

"Just try," she urged, and reached across the table to him, palm up, offering a gentle, physical touch.

He slid his hand into hers, the contact between them warm, solid, and intimate. "This past week has been hell," he admitted gruffly. "And while you going to work goes against my need to take care of you, in every way, I realized after hanging up the phone with you last night just how selfish I was being. You've given me so much and have never asked for anything just for yourself, until now. And I reacted defensively, because what *you* want goes against the man I thought I needed to be."

She remained silent, shocked that he'd come to those conclusions, but relieved that he was opening up to her in ways he never had before.

He swallowed hard and continued. "You know what my childhood was like. You know all the guilt and regrets I have over my mother's abuse and suicide. You know how much I despised my father and how I hated that he was never man enough to take care of me and my mother. I swore I would *never* be like him, that I'd always take care of you and the boys and make sure you wanted for nothing."

"And we never have," she said, giving his hand a squeeze, her own heart tightening in her chest at his raw, emotional confession. "You've given us a great life, Dean."

"I know." He gave her a slight smile that didn't reach his eyes. "But over the past few months you've become this confident, independent woman, and when it comes to you and me together sexually, I fucking love it. Last night, you blew my mind and I'm still reeling, but coming to terms with you being confident and independent and wanting to work, I was struck with this awful fear that if you had a job that was new and exciting, you wouldn't need me any longer." He winced, as if he regretted giving her that vulnerable glimpse into his soul.

She stood up, then sat down on Dean's lap, wanting to be close to him, wanting him to look directly into her eyes when she laid herself bare for him, too. She framed his face in her hands, knowing with every fiber of her being that her life would cease to exist without this man in it. "I will *always* need you, Dean," she said, brushing her thumbs across his cheeks, while his hand slipped into the opening of her robe and tenderly caressed her thigh. "You are my husband, my best friend, my heart and soul. That will *never* change."

He closed his eyes for a moment, his big body shuddering in what felt like relief to Jillian.

"I know you like to be in control of everything, that you like things to be smooth and predictable," she said, trying to inject a bit of humor into her tone. "This is just one small bump in the road and I'm sure there will be more. We're going to disagree, and we need to talk it through when that happens. But I really do want this job, and knowing that I have your support means everything to me."

"You have it. I swear," he said, his voice vibrating with sincerity. "I want you to be happy, Jillian. You *deserve* to be happy, to do what you love, and I'm sorry I was such an ass about it."

That's all she needed to hear to know that she had her husband's blessing.

A sexy idea popped into her mind, and she untied her sash as she gave Dean a sly smile. "Yes, you were a bit of an ass," she teased, and shrugged the robe off her shoulders so it fell down her arms, exposing her breasts and already taut nipples to his heated gaze. "I'm thinking maybe you need to make it up to me, earn my forgiveness, and show me just how contrite and apologetic you are."

Clearly up for the challenge, he stood up and hoisted her over his shoulder in his favorite caveman style, then strode to the bedroom, dropped her onto the big, king-sized bed, and proceeded to apologize in the most erotic and creative ways.

EPILOGUE

Raina Beck finished helping a customer select a bottle of warming massage oil, that was also cinnamon flavored for added fun, and headed over into the lingerie section of Sugar Spice, where Jillian was perusing the rack of new arrivals.

"Find anything you like?" Raina asked as the other woman contemplated a leopard print bustier before putting it back on the stand.

Jillian smiled at her as she shuffled through a few more items. "The problem is, there's too much to like, which is a good thing. I'm looking for something a little different than everything I already have . . ." Her words trailed off, and her eyes lit up as she lifted a hanger displaying a sexy red ensemble that consisted of a demi bra, a short flirty skirt that was only a few inches of fabric that would barely cover her bottom, and a matching lace thong, along with a garter belt and thigh-high stockings.

"I think this is it," Jillian announced with a succinct nod of her head.

"If Dean comes home to find you wearing that outfit, I think all bets are off," Raina teased her friend.

"That's what I'm counting on, and I think he'll really like the short little skirt, too." She handed the hanger to Raina. "I'll take it, along with one of those feather ticklers you have on display, the one with the soft ostrich feathers."

"You got it." Raina selected a tickler with deep red feathers to match the outfit, and met Raina up at the front counter. She rang in her purchases and asked, "How are you enjoying working with Stephanie?"

"I absolutely love it. I couldn't be happier," Jillian said, her expression reflecting her newfound joy. "I'm helping her design those fantasy suites at the hotel, and tomorrow I have a consultation with a woman who wants to redecorate her bedroom in a sexier version theme of The Secret Garden."

"Sounds like a fun project." Raina swiped Jillian's credit card to process the sale. The two of them had become good friends, and because she knew Jillian's husband had been so opposed to his wife taking a job, Raina couldn't help but wonder how that was going. "Is everything still good with Dean and you working for Stephanie?"

"He's getting used to it and adjusting. I make sure I always have time for just the two of us, and it keeps him happy."

"Men really are such basic creatures," Raina said with a laugh. "Keep them plied with food and sex and they're happy, content and satisfied."

Jillian lifted a curious brow. "Speaking of men and sex . . . when are *you* going to indulge a little?"

Raina shrugged as she wrapped her

ensemble in pink tissue and tucked it into a bag. "I think all the good guys are taken. And then there's the men that find out I own a sex toy boutique and decide I'm fair game for outrageous, kinky sexy, because, you know, I have access to all sorts of depraved items."

"Maybe you need hot *anonymous* sex," Jillian suggested with a naughty twinkle in her eye.

"It's been a long, dry spell and the idea is definitely tempting," Raina replied, a humorous note lacing the truth of her words. Vibrators and sex toys did the job as far as getting her off, but it couldn't replace the feel or pleasure of a strong, powerful, virile man thrusting deep inside of her, or having his hands skimming along her curves, his mouth seducing hers.

Yes, she definitely missed that, and the provocative thought made her feel a bit flushed.

Jillian bit her bottom lip for a second before reaching into her purse and pulling out a white envelope. "You've done a lot for me, and I want to do something for you for a change. Take this, and indulge yourself." She pushed the envelope across the counter to Raina.

Frowning, Raina picked it up and read the word, *Welcome*, embossed in black across the front. "What is this?" she asked, confused and curious at the same time.

"An invitation to The Players Club."

Want to know what happens to Raina at The Players Club? Read on for a sneak peek excerpt to PLAYING WITH TEMPTATION.

Other Books in
The Marriage Diaries Series
THE MARRIAGE DIARIES
THE INVITATION
THE CAPTURE

PLAYING WITH
TEMPTATION

TEMPTATION HAS NEVER BEEN SO HOT...

When Raina Beck is given an invitation to The Players Club, all she wants is a night of decadence with a gorgeous, sexy stranger. The seductive, mysterious man she meets fulfills her deepest desires and most erotic fantasics, giving her a night she'll never forget. But forgetting *him* isn't quite so easy.

Logan Cruz prefers his women submissive and compliant in the bedroom . . . everything the independent Raina is not. Yet from the first moment he lays eyes on her, he's determined to make Raina his. Despite her resistance.

When Logan is assigned to protect Raina from a stalker, everything between them changes. Sex becomes more than just physical, and emotions run deep. Falling in love was never on Raina's agenda, but can she let go of the past and surrender the one thing he wants the most . . . her heart?

CHAPTER ONE EXCERPT

Raina Beck finished helping a customer select a bottle of warming massage oil, then headed over to the lingerie section of her store, Sugar and Spice, a sensual, upscale adult boutique that catered to the residents of San Diego. She paused at the rack of new arrivals, where her good friend, Jillian Noble, was perusing the gorgeous items.

"Find anything you like?" Raina asked as the other woman contemplated a leopard print bustier before putting it back on the stand.

Jillian smiled at her as she shuffled through a few more pieces. "The problem is, there's too much to like, which is a good thing. I'm looking for something a little different than everything I already have . . ." Her words trailed off, and her eyes lit up as she lifted a hanger displaying a sexy red ensemble that consisted of a demi bra, a short flirty skirt that was only a few inches of fabric that would barely cover her bottom, and a matching lace thong, along with a garter belt and thigh-high stockings.

"I think this is it," Jillian announced with a succinct nod of her head.

"If Dean comes home to find you wearing that outfit, I think all bets are off," Raina teased her friend.

"That's what I'm counting on, and I think he'll really like the short little skirt, too." She handed the hanger to Raina. "I'll take it, along with one of those feather ticklers you have on display, the one with the soft ostrich feathers."

"You got it." Raina smiled, knowing Jillian, a good customer, appreciated the more sexually adventurous items Sugar and Spice provided to those who wanted to kink up their sex lives. Selecting a tickler with deep red feathers to match the outfit, she met her friend up at the front counter.

As she rang up Jillian's purchases, she asked, "How are you enjoying working with Stephanie?"

"I absolutely love it. I couldn't be happier," Jillian said, her expression reflecting her newfound joy. "I'm helping her design those fantasy suites at the hotel, and tomorrow I have a consultation with a woman who wants to redecorate her bedroom in a sexier version theme of The Secret Garden."

"Sounds like a fun project." Raina swiped Jillian's credit card to process the sale. The two of them had become close friends over the past months, and because she knew Jillian's husband had been so opposed to his wife taking a job, Raina couldn't help but wonder how that was going. "Is everything still good with Dean and you working for Stephanie?"

"He's getting used to it and adjusting. I make sure I always have time for just the two of us, and it keeps him happy."

"Men really are such basic creatures,"

Raina said with a laugh. "Keep them plied with food and sex and they're happy, content, and satisfied."

Jillian lifted a curious brow. "Speaking of men and sex . . . when are *you* going to indulge a little?"

Raina shrugged as she wrapped her ensemble in pink tissue and tucked it into a bag. "I think all the good guys are taken. And then there's the men that find out I own a sex toy boutique and decide I'm fair game for outrageous, kinky sex, because, you know, I have access to all sorts of depraved items."

She rolled her eyes to make light of her comment, but the truth ran much deeper and stirred up other painful memories that reminded her of why she kept her heart and emotions under lock and key—the pain of such complete and utter rejection was something that had left her guarded, and very cautious when it came to a man's interest in her.

Admittedly, she *did* enjoy hot, adventurous sex. After all, she'd opened Sugar and Spice as a way to help women empower themselves sexually, to get in touch with their desires and be confident enough to enjoy every aspect of sex. But she also knew it took an equally strong, self-assured man to accept her line of business, to not feel threatened or embarrassed by the fact that she owned a boutique that catered to enhancing sexual pleasure.

Unfortunately, over the years she'd learned that she wasn't the best judge of character when it came to a man's motives and his reasons for dating her, which also made it extremely difficult to decipher what was *real*, or if she was nothing more than someone's dirty little secret that they used until the excitement wore off.

Too many painful experiences had taught her that because of what she did for a living, men were more than willing to fuck her like a porn star in private, but they drew the line at taking her out in public, or bringing her home to meet the family, which made her feel cheap and dirty—as if her own father's fire and brimstone prediction about her being a whore had come true. Men didn't date *a woman like her* with long term in mind, and it had become much easier for Raina to keep her emotional distance rather than face criticism and the sting of rejection all over again.

She'd been burned a few times, and she wasn't allowing any man to get close enough to do it again. Now, sex was all about physical pleasure, nothing more, and she'd recently decided that if anyone was going to do the *using*, it was going to be *her* for a change. Unfortunately, an opportunity hadn't presented itself, but if the right guy came along, she certainly wasn't opposed to enjoying a no-strings-attached, one-night-stand.

"Maybe you need hot *anonymous* sex," Jillian suggested with a naughty twinkle in her eye, as if she'd had a direct link to Raina's thoughts.

"It's been a long, dry spell and the idea is definitely tempting," Raina replied, a humorous note lacing the truth of her words. Vibrators and sex toys did the job as far as getting her off, but it couldn't replace the feel or pleasure of a strong, powerful, virile man thrusting deep inside of her, or having his hands skimming along her curves, his hot mouth seducing hers.

Yes, she definitely missed that, and the provocative thought made her feel a bit flushed.

Jillian bit her bottom lip for a second before reaching into her purse and pulling out a white envelope. "You've done a lot for me, and I want to do something for you for a change. Take this, and indulge yourself." She pushed the envelope across the counter to Raina.

Raina picked it up and read the word, *Welcome*, embossed in black across the front. "What is this?" she asked, confused and curious at the same time.

"An invitation to The Players Club."

Raina's eyes widened in surprise, and her heart fluttered in her chest with undeniable excitement. She knew exactly what The Players Club was—a private, members-only sex club that catered to an elite and prominent clientele in order to maintain its exclusivity. A personal recommendation was required to even visit the club, and since Dean and Jillian had recently become members, they now had the privilege of extending an invitation to a guest.

And Jillian had chosen *her*.

"Oh, wow," Raina breathed as she brushed her thumb over the embossed lettering on the envelope, still in shock. "Really?"

"Yes, *really*," Jillian mimicked playfully. "You deserve a sexy night all to yourself, and I can guarantee that *any* fantasy you have can be fulfilled at The Players Club."

Raina had plenty of private, naughty fantasies stored away in the deepest recesses of her mind, none of which she'd ever shared because those scenarios were just too wicked and forbidden to reveal to any of the guys she'd dated up to this point, all of whom had big egos and had been self-centered lovers. Yes, she owned a boutique that sold all sorts of kinky items to enhance sex play, but it took a strong, confident man who didn't feel threatened by her expertise to give her what she desired, who knew what she needed without asking and made that pleasure his sole focus.

Finding that kind of compelling man at The Players Club in one night was improbable but certainly more possible than in her daily life, and she wasn't about to refuse Jillian's gift. She'd been given the equivalent of Willy Wonka's golden ticket, but instead of gorging on chocolate, she planned to indulge in as many orgasms as she could.

CHAPTER TWO EXCERPT

Two weeks later...

Raina wasn't sure what to expect once she arrived at The Players Club, but as she stared up at the huge, sprawling, three-story mansion that had been built on the side of the mountain and over-looked the city of Fallbrook below, she was certainly impressed by the gorgeous, majestic looking house. At night, the place was illuminated by low-profile lighting, and the Mediterranean architectural style was warm and inviting. From the outside, there was absolutely nothing to indicate that this place was actually a club that catered to those who preferred taking a walk on the wilder side of sex.

Excitement and anticipation swirled inside of her as a young valet took the keys to her car, slid into her vehicle, and drove away. Holding just her invitation in her hand, she inhaled a deep, fortifying breath and climbed the stairs that led to a luxurious open courtyard, where a few couples were standing around, conversing and enjoying the cool summer evening before heading inside for more illicit indoor activities. One of the men in the group glanced at Raina as she headed toward the entrance, and their gazes met since she'd been casually looking his way, too.

As a woman who owned a sex shop, she'd learned to look people directly in the eye, without shame, embarrassment, or judgment. It also showed confidence and that skill came in handy now. The man staring back at her was nice looking enough, and though she wasn't attracted to him in any way, she gave him an amicable smile, the kind she'd offer a customer in her store to break the ice and let them know she was friendly and approachable.

A lascivious grin curved his mouth as he gave her a very thorough and blatant once-over, his gaze raking down the little black dress that hugged her curves and ended mid-thigh. His appraisal kept going, traveling all the way down her long legs to the rhinestone studded strappy stilettos on her feet, and back up again to the thick, blond hair she'd left down in soft, tumbling waves around her shoulders.

His gaze, when it returned to hers, was heated and undeniably interested. Unfortunately, he didn't do a thing for her libido and didn't even register as a tiny blip on her sexual radar. It was then that Raina decided that if she was going to have any kind of physical contact with a guy tonight, she wanted off-the-charts combustible chemistry to accompany it. The kind of instantaneous lust that made her hot and wet with just a glance. The kind of excitement that made her entire body sizzle with electricity before he even touched her.

Not just anyone would do. Yes, she was

setting her standards extremely high, but she'd rather go home to her battery-operated boyfriend then settle for a mediocre encounter that left her wanting more, anyways. Tonight was all about going for the gusto, taking risks, and reaping the kind of pleasure she'd denied herself for much too long.

"I don't think I've ever seen her here before," the man who'd been ogling her mused to the other couple with him, loud enough for Raina to hear as she walked past. "And you know how I enjoy breaking in the newbies."

The woman snorted inelegantly. "Contrary to what you might believe, not every woman enjoys being bound, gagged, and flogged."

"I've been known to change a woman's mind," he drawled arrogantly. "And just for the record, I use the softest, most supple leather available on the market. Women love the way it feels on their skin. I've yet to have anyone complain."

The man clearly had a giant-sized ego, and if he'd intended to excite her with his knowledge of whips and floggers, she wasn't at all impressed, considering she sold those items in her store. Truthfully, she wouldn't mind a man who gave a bit of calculated pain with her pleasure, but there was a level of trust that needed to be established first, and she'd never allow a stranger that kind of privilege.

With that in mind, she was grateful that The Players Club abided by the safe, sane, and consensual rules, which had been stated in the guest contract she'd signed, including a two drink maximum and zero-tolerance policy on drug use of any sort to make certain decision were made without any undue influence.

The standard safe word to stop any sort of sex play was *red*, and if it was ever ignored the person who didn't heed the warning was immediately expelled and banned from the club. Jillian had assured her that there were attendants throughout the place to maintain all aspects of a guest's safety, and then there was also the confidential background security check and health screening everyone had to pass before their first visit. The discreet guidelines were set in place to maintain and preserve the integrity of the club and they took those rules very seriously.

Raina continued toward the entrance, and just as she reached the giant-sized double front doors to the mansion, they opened and a young woman greeted Raina with a smile. Once she was inside the gorgeous and elegant lobby, Raina handed the young woman her invitation.

The hostess introduced herself as Lise and once she'd checked Raina's name on the approved list, she proceeded to give her the first-timers spiel about *what* was located *where*. From the viewing rooms upstairs, to the open playrooms and themed fantasy boudoirs, to the dungeon and the Thursday evening *Rave* party down on the lower level of the mansion, and everything else in between.

"You can start in the Player's Lounge where you can mingle, which is right that way," Lise indicated with a wave of her hand. "Or you can go ahead and explore the mansion, stop where you want, and indulge as you wish."

Raina wasn't one for small-talk and pick-up lines, not in a situation like this. Whatever happened, with whoever it happened with, she wanted it to develop naturally, so she opted for the latter. "I think I'd like to explore and see what my options are."

"Go right ahead," Lise said, then turned toward another couple who'd just entered the club, leaving Raina on her own.

Just as she stepped into the main entry hall, a neatly dressed waiter arrived with a tray of champagne flutes. "Would you like something to drink?"

Champagne sounded lovely, and she accepted one of the glasses. "Yes, thank you."

She took a sip of the sweetened sparkling wine as she contemplated the split staircase that led toward two separate wings of the house, along with the directional signs informing patrons that the public viewing rooms were to the right, and the private rooms were to the left.

Another wide stairway led down to the area below designated "The Dungeon", where tonight's Rave party was also being held.

She headed up to the public viewing rooms first, taking in the plethora of sexual activities going on all around her, fascinated by everyone's lack of inhibition. Couples were openly having sex while others watched, and some even joined in on the fun. There were public spankings and orgies going on, and different themed rooms offered to fulfill fantasies that involved all sorts of kinky scenarios. She viewed some interesting fetishes, including watching as a dominatrix made a tied-up man drop to his knees and lick her leather, spike-heeled boots while she whipped him with a crop.

Men and women walked by her, some even touching her bare arm or back—a light caress that expressed interest without aggression. Even though her senses were saturated with all things sex-related, no one in particular appealed to her enough to accept their silent offers, though she did find all the various scenes and sights highly arousing.

Maybe she was more of a voyeur than an exhibitionist, she mused as she finished her champagne and set the empty glass on a table before deciding to see what the Dungeon was all about. She took the stairs to the lowest level of the mansion, and it did, indeed, feel very much like a dungeon down below, with wall scones providing a muted red illumination. Shackles and chains hung from the walls and ceilings, and the darkened chamber was also equipped with a few St. Andrew's crosses, along with all sorts of benches, cages, stocks and swings.

Currently in progress were bondage scenes, slavery, and resistance play, and each scene drew a crowd of on-lookers, while dungeon monitors stood nearby, supervising scenes to make sure everything remained safe and consensual. A man in leather chaps used a rope on another well-built man, tying his wrists and arms together behind him in the most intricate way, almost like an art form, before grabbing a handful of the bound man's hair and forcing the guy to suck him off.

Riveted by the erotic sight of two such masculine men together, Raina felt a flush of heat suffuse her entire body. The act was primal and raw and wholly sexual, and holy shit, the man's dominance over his partner was so freakin' hot it left her breathless.

Between the glass of champagne and the scene she'd just witnessed, her body was buzzing. Her sex throbbed, and her nipples peaked and scraped against the lace of her bra. It was like watching live porn, the scent and sounds echoing off the chamber's walls adding to the titillating and X-rated atmosphere.

She moved on to another less-crowded performance, showcasing a gentleman in a tailored suit bringing his "secretary" to heel. The woman was bent over a large desk, her arms bound, a ball gag in her mouth, and the man was smacking her ass with a wide leather paddle. Her skin was a bright stinging shade of pink, but with every swat of the paddle she moaned and thrashed in the throes of pleasure, clearly loving the punishment.

"Like what you see?"

The low, masculine voice so close to her ear startled Raina. She turned her head and met the steady brown gaze of the man she'd seen out in the courtyard. She couldn't help but wonder how long he'd been following her throughout the club, watching her . . . and didn't care for the unsettling sensation in her stomach—even though he hadn't done anything to pose any kind of threat to her.

"Umm, I'm just . . . browsing," she said as non-committally as she could manage, even as she realized how silly that sounded in a *sex club*.

He tipped his head, his interest in her unmistakable. "Maybe I could persuade you to participate in a scene of our own?" he suggested.

She shook her head and gave him a placating smile. "No, thank you."

He raised an arrogant, dark-blonde brow. "I can give you a whole lot of pleasure to offset the pain," he persisted, and stroked a hand down her bare back.

She sucked in a breath, not appreciating that he'd taken such an intimate liberty when she'd made it very clear she wasn't attracted to him, or his offer. Looking him straight in the eye, she said the word *"red"* very firmly, and loudly enough for a nearby dungeon monitor to hear.

The too-cocky man immediately obeyed the safe word and stopped touching her. With an irritable scowl on his face, his raised his hands up, and the supervisor stepped away again, satisfied that he'd complied.

His jaw clenched indignantly. "Jesus, that was a bit extreme."

"I just wanted to make it very clear that I have no desire in being gagged, bound, and flogged," she said evenly. "By you, or anyone else here."

"You really should try it. You might like it," he said, and smirked. "In fact, I'd bet money I could make you come better and harder than you ever have."

Oh, puleeze. She just barely refrained

from rolling her eyes. Obviously, she'd bruised his fragile ego and he felt the need to compensate. "Gamble your money elsewhere," she said very sweetly. "I'm really not interested; therefore *you* making me *come*, in any capacity, isn't going to happen."

His gaze narrowed ever-so-slightly at her wise-crack, but he'd pushed and he'd deserved the verbal smack-down. Unwilling to engage with him further, she walked away and headed down an adjoining corridor, following the sound of electronic techno music until she reached the opposite end of the mansion where the Thursday night Rave party was being held. The huge, open area was designed to look like an underground warehouse, with laser light shows, erotic images projected onto the bare walls, and smoke machines adding to the sultry, sex-infused mood.

She glanced behind her, and satisfied that Mr. Bound and Gag wasn't anywhere to be seen, she moved into the fray of people. A lot of the men were shirtless, the women scantily clothed, making her feel overly covered in her dress and heels, even though she had plenty of skin showing. Most everyone was dancing like bohemians, without modesty or propriety. This is where the epitome of dirty dancing was defined, with men and women grinding and writhing against one another, unbridled in their passion and pursuit of pleasure.

A few men and women reached out to touch her, to draw her into the ribald revelry, but she managed to evade getting swept into the gyrating, groping mass of people. Because she didn't want to get caught up in one of the many orgies going on, she veered off toward a stage, where half a dozen life-size, gold-gilded bird cages were displayed and overlooked the rest of the room. A few of them were occupied, mostly with couples dancing and humping and groping one another. Feeling like she'd be the safest in one of those barred enclosures by herself, Raina made her way to the stage, then up the five small steps to enter one of the vacant gilded cages. She latched the lock from the inside, just to make sure she had no surprise visitors.

She took a moment to look around, to take in her view from her perch above everything and everyone. Besides the enormous dance floor, there was also a large lounge area with private chairs and couches for those who wanted more creature comforts, and right below the stage was a bar serving guests their two-drink minimum and bottles of water.

Feeling secure in her own little coop, it was easy to let the pulsing beat of the music infuse her body, inviting her to let go of her own inhibitions. She loved to dance, and she grabbed onto the stripper-like pole in the center of the cage and did a little dirty dancing of her own. She'd taken pole-dancing classes with her girlfriends, and it was incredibly liberating and freeing to wrap her calf around the pole, arch her back, and execute a graceful, sensual twirl that made her feel confident and incredibly sexy.

Closing her eyes, she let the provocative sway of her body sync with the rhythmic tempo of the music. After a few more erotic moves, including a few shimmies, gyrations, and a hair toss for good measure, she opened her eyes and glanced down, realizing that she'd drawn a small but avid crowd at the base of the stage—which so had not been her intent.

But out of all those men staring up at her, it was the stunningly gorgeous one sitting at the bar below who'd clearly been watching her performance that set her heart beating hard and fast in her chest. Even with the distance separating them, even through the haze and flashing lights, his intense, hungry gaze captured her attention and made her skin prickle in awareness. A frisson of lust shot through her veins, and her sex clenched with a desire so strong she could feel the slick heat and moisture gathering between her thighs.

Completely enthralled by the undeniable chemistry vibrating between them, she let her lashes fall half-mast and gave him a sultry, come-hither smile as she continued to dance around the pole, moving her body slowly, sinuously, temptingly. He never looked away, never turned his head to acknowledge the woman who'd come up beside him and was doing her best to try and distract him with the surgically enhanced breasts nearly spilling out of her top.

Raina couldn't tear her gaze away from him, either. She licked her bottom lip, suddenly knowing without a doubt that *he* was the one she wanted tonight.

As if he'd read her mind, he pushed away from the bar and started through the crowd, his stride purposeful and predatory as he made his way to the stage—and she felt very much like a bird in a gilded cage, being stalked by a lithe, untamed panther. But instead of any sort of fear, her pulse raced with a heady anticipation, and the excitement building inside her made her feel wild and reckless.

He reached the raised platform and climbed the stairs that led to her cage, then stopped right in front of the door that led inside. She leaned back against the steel pole, taking him in—and oh, Lord, there was a whole lot of man to admire.

His hair was a dark shade of brown, cut short but tousled just enough to make her fingers itch to run through those soft-looking strands. Even wearing a black silk shirt and black pants, there was no denying the width of his shoulders and just how well-built the rest of his body was beneath his clothes. In a flash of strobe light, she could see the hard, unmistakable ridge of his cock outlined against the front of his pants.

Her mouth went dry, her stomach muscles clenched in need, and she raised her gaze all the way back up to the bad boy glint in those bright green eyes. Standing just a few feet away, he was tall and commanding, sexually confident, and a prime example of the word *fuckable*.

Her knees went weak at the decadent thought.

He didn't force his way into the cage. Didn't try to reach in and flip the lock himself. Clearly a man used to getting his way, he only had to ask for what he wanted, and he didn't hesitate to let his desires be known.

Let me in.

She read the words that formed on his full, sensual lips, knowing that the moment she obeyed his request and allowed him inside the cage with her—*and she knew she would*—that all bets were off and this man would claim her, here and now.

Oh, yes please.

Stepping up to the locked door, she opened it for him, inviting him inside. He was so tall he had to duck through the entryway, and once he straightened to his full height again he immediately backed her up against the side of the cage, aligning the hard length of his body firmly against hers, pinning her there in the most delicious, delightful way.

His gaze bore into hers, flashing with carnal lust. His scent—spicy after-shave and male pheromones—intoxicated her. Everything about him generated so much heat, she felt like she was burning up from the inside out. Wanting to touch him, desperate to feel all that raw power he exuded, she placed her hands on his chest, the soft material of his shirt contradicting the rock-hard muscles flexing beneath the fabric.

Against her palm, she felt his chest rumble, right before he grabbed both of her wrists and lifted her arms above her head. He curled her fingers around the metal bars to grip them tight, making it very clear without speaking a word that he was a man who liked to be in control.

Normally, *she* was the one in control sexually and liked having the upper hand, so there was no chance of letting down her guard with a man and allowing them to have that much power over her mind and body. But tonight was all about stealing as much pleasure as she could with a man she'd never see again. And if he preferred to be in charge, she wasn't about to complain, because there was something incredibly thrilling about this man's very dominant nature in a place like The Players Club, where indulging in the forbidden and erotic was expected.

The techno music matched the frantic beat of her pulse as he pressed a knee between her legs and used his feet to push her own wide apart and keep them spread. His hips gyrated against hers in a slow, tantalizing, grinding dance that made her ache for a more intimate touch and deeper penetration. His sinful gaze watched her every response, tracking the rapid rise and fall of her breasts beneath her dress and the way she shamelessly arched her back for a closer, tighter fit.

Intensity radiated from him, and a faint hint of satisfaction touched his mouth, giving her a glimpse of something darker and far more wicked. Lifting a hand, he slid it into her hair and fisted his fingers in the long blonde strands so she felt the slight stinging tug against her scalp, then pulled her head back so that her face was tipped up to his.

Her lips parted on a gasp, and he took advantage and kissed her, his lips hard and unrelenting as they captured hers. He licked his way into her mouth, gradually deepening the stroke of his tongue against hers, completely consuming her with his kiss. His free hand touched her thigh, his fingers brazenly caressing their way beneath the hem of her dress and up the inside of her leg, until he reached the silky barrier covering her mound.

She groaned into his ravaging mouth and clutched the bars above her head as he boldly pressed two fingers against her throbbing sex, rubbed along those swollen nether lips and unerringly found her aching clit beneath the scrap of lingerie. She was drenched with arousal, her panties soaked with the need for release as he continued to stroke her like a man who knew his way around a woman's body. He could have teased her, could have easily kept her on that sharp edge of ecstasy, but instead he pushed her right over that steep crest so that she was free-falling into a stunning, explosive climax that left her panting against his lips and her legs shaking.

The blissful orgasm should have satisfied her, but instead made her crave more. Made her frantic to feel this sexy, dominant man filling her, hard and deep.

He leaned in close, brushing his lips against the shell of her ear. "Now I'm going to fuck you," he rasped, the gruff, guttural tone of his voice making her shiver.

The whispered promise was her undoing. "*Yes*," she replied. *Anywhere, and anyway he wanted.*

She expected him to take her right there in the cage, up against the metal bars, and she would have been fine with that. But instead, he grabbed her hand and led her out of the pen, down the stage and toward the far end of the room where there were couches and chairs and other more comfortable pieces of furniture in different alcoves. He chose a vacant corner with a big, over-stuffed chair and pulled a curtain around their little area.

The drapery was white, thin, and sheer, giving them only the barest illusion of privacy. Anyone who wanted to watch them could. Raina realized she'd gone from voyeur to exhibitionist, and with this man she was beyond caring. She didn't know anyone here, would never return or see this man again, and she was at a *sex* club, for heaven's sake. It was all a part of the experience, and she wanted to fulfill this erotic fantasy.

When she turned back around to face him, the sizzling burn in his eyes was nearly her undoing. Every line of his body was rigid and taut, as if he was waiting for her to make the next move, to make sure that this was what she wanted. She hadn't expected that kind of courtesy from him, either, but a part of her appreciated the gesture.

No guts, no glory, no pleasure. Let's do this. She was meeting with her girlfriends in the morning, and she'd promised them the juicy details. No way was she going to disappoint them with anything but a spectacular encounter with a sex God of a man.

Splaying her hands on his chest, she pushed him back, until his strong legs hit the seat and he had nowhere else to go but to sit down. He plopped into the chair, an amused smile on his lips—though she got the distinct impression that he was just humoring her for the moment and her having any kind of upper hand was only a temporary reprieve. Spreading his legs wide, he sat forward and grasped her hips, drawing her in between his thighs before slipping both of his big, warm hands beneath the hem of her dress.

Grasping the waistband of her panties, he pulled them down her legs. She braced her hands on his shoulders as he helped her step out of the lacy underwear, then he stuffed the scrap of fabric into his pocket. He quickly unbuttoned his pants, freeing the thick length of his erection, giving her a few seconds to admire his gorgeous cock as he grabbed one of the foil packets in the crystal bowl on a table beside the chair, ripped it open with his teeth, and quickly put the condom on.

He hooked his fingers behind her knees, guiding her forward onto the chair so that she was straddling his lap and the engorged head of his erection slid along her wet cleft and tucked tight against her opening. Hands clutching her hips beneath the bunched up material of her dress, he lifted his gaze to hers, his eyes speaking a language her body instinctively understood.

I'm going to sink inside you so hard and deep, you won't ever forget I was here.

She believed him. Her head fell back and her breath caught in her lungs as he brought her down on his shaft in one smooth, firm thrust that filled her to the brink of pain. It had been a long time since she'd been with a man, and none of the penis-shaped vibrators in her nightstand drawer even came close to the shocking size and width of his cock.

That delicious burn quickly gave way to a greater pleasure as her body adjusted to accommodate him as he drove into her, again and again, the steady pump of his hips matching the rhythmic beat of the music pulsing around them. She fisted her hands in his shirt, so very tempted to rip open the buttons to look and touch, to lick and taste his smooth, taut skin. To revel in everything about this assertive, fascinating man so that the memories of this evening with him would be branded in her mind forever.

Giving into the urge, her fingers fumbled with the top button to unfasten his shirt, but he let go of her hips and caught her wrists in his hands. Just like in the cage, he pulled her hands away and secured her arms behind her back, his long, strong fingers manacling her as effectively as a pair of handcuffs would. The position forced her shoulders back, caused her spine to arch and the swollen breasts confined beneath her dress ache to be freed.

This alpha man was definitely all about dominance, and she was shocked to realized just how much being restrained by him turned her on . . . as well as the fact that they were being watched by others in the club through the sheer, gauzy curtain. They were both still decently covered, but there was no mistaking the joining of their bodies or what they were doing, and a part of her wished that they were naked so she could feel the heat of his chest against her hardened nipples, his muscled stomach flexing against her belly, her quivering thighs sliding against his hair-roughened ones.

The strobe lights flashed, accentuating his masculine features, the smoky hue of his eyes, the clench of his jaw as he continued to piston her up and down on his cock, fucking her long, and hard, and so damned good. He possessed and claimed, their coupling hot and raw and primitive.

Somehow, he managed to wrap the fingers of one of his hands around both of her small wrists, keeping her arms pinned, while his free hand dipped down between her spread legs. He grazed her burgeoning clit with his fingers, ripping a shuddering moan from her. He played her expertly, the unyielding pressure of his thumb stroking that bundle of nerves pitching her closer and closer to a combustible orgasm.

Through hooded lashes, he watched her ride him, watched as the explosion brewing inside of her gathered, threatening to send her up in flames. Watched as she completely unraveled and came apart for him with a soft cry of ecstasy. Her internal muscles gripped his cock, clenched him tight, giving her a small sense of power as he surged his hips upward, ramming home, his erratic thrusts signaling his own climax.

His head fell back, his irises deepening

to a darker shade of green. She read the words, "*oh, fuck*" that formed on his lips as his big body stiffened as he came, and his hips bucked hard against hers, leaving every inch of her flesh tender and sensitive and undeniably marked.

Boneless and utterly sated, she collapsed against his chest, her face buried against his warm, fragrant neck as she tried to get her bearings back on track. He finally released her hands, and she groaned as she brought her arms back around, trying to ease the delicious ache in her shoulders from having them restrained for too long. He skimmed a flattened palm up her spine, his touch light and gentle, a direct, startling contrast to the demanding man who'd just ravished her.

Long fingers tangled in her hair, then pulled her head back so he could look down at her face. He was frowning, and for a moment she fully expected him to tell her to get off of him so he could be on his way—she had no idea what the protocol for this sort of thing was and she hadn't meant to come across as clingy—but he didn't seem anxious to part ways.

"Are you okay?" he asked, loud enough to be heard above the music.

She hadn't anticipated his concern, either—certainly not in a place like this where a little rough play was common. Expected and encouraged even. His ability to command her body so thoroughly just moments ago, then switch gears to check on her mental and physical well-being changed everything about him—made him go from a hard-core sex object to something far more dangerous and appealing and *real*.

Not caring for the sudden heavy beating of her heart, she pushed away from his chest and gave him a reassuring smile that contradicted the odd twinge of regret forming in her chest. "I'm good."

She lied, and he didn't look completely convinced, either. That he even *cared* was something totally unexpected and confusing to her, and she needed distance to clear her head and put things back into proper perspective.

She used the best excuse she could think of. "Where is the ladies' room?"

"Over by the bar, just past the men's room," he said, jutting his jaw in that general direction.

"Thanks." Slowly, she stood, trying not to groan as their bodies separated—and very aware of the fact that he was still semi-hard. She straightened the hem of her dress and turned to go, but he caught her wrist and stopped her. Her pulse tripped all over itself—and she honestly hated that a man she'd just met had that much power over her self-control when she'd been so determined to treat tonight like a fun, no-strings-attached fling.

She glanced back at him, relieved to see that sexy, bad boy smile of his making an appearance. The bad boy she could handle more than the caring man.

"I'll meet you back here," he drawled, looking so freakin' irresistible Raina had to resist the urge not to climb back onto his lap right then and there. "I'm not done with you yet."

His words were casual and flirtatious,

but coming from a man like him, there was no doubt in her mind that they were more an order than a request. One she was certain that any other woman wouldn't hesitate to obey, knowing the kind of pleasure he was capable of giving.

She made no promises, just walked on very shaky legs toward the women's restroom. She used the facilities, washed her hands, then paused in the lounge area, where a few other women were sitting around and talking. Her legs still felt like wet noodles and her mind was still spinning, so she sat down in a chair off to the side. There was a counter in front of her, with a long, full-length mirror, and Raina stared at her reflection, shocked by what she saw—a woman who'd been well and truly fucked.

Her hair was a tousled mess from his hands, her blue eyes a bit dreamy from two amazing orgasms. Her skin was flushed, and her mouth was pink and swollen. She licked her bottom lip, still tasting him there, and dear Lord, she wanted *more* of him.

Nothing and no one would ever compare to what she'd just experienced—the attraction and off-the-charts chemistry between them, and the way he'd so instinctively mastered her body and tapped into her deepest, darkest desires, the ones she'd never shared with any other man before. It was a sobering thought that struck a slice of panic inside of her, because she feared he was a man she could easily get addicted to. A man who could tear down her guard and melt her resolve to keep every emotional component *out* of sex.

She exhaled a deep breath and mentally shored up her fortitude to get out of this situation as gracefully as possible. To her favor, he knew nothing about her. Not her past, her present life, nothing. She had to admit that it had been so nice to have that anonymity, without any expectations, just mutual pleasure. And that's exactly how she wanted to keep tonight's encounter—as a hot tryst between strangers. Her emotional well-being depended on it.

Now, she just had to figure out how to leave the club without running into him again, because one touch and she knew her willpower to resist him would crumble.

She stepped out of the ladies' room and glanced in the direction of the alcove they'd shared, relieved to find the area vacant. Assuming he'd made a similar trip to the men's room, Raina dodged her way through the throng of people still enjoying the Rave, and toward the stairs leading to the upper level of the mansion. She reached the entryway without incident, and continued out the main doors to the courtyard, then to the valet.

It was quiet outside compared to all the action going on inside the club, and as she waited for one of the attendants to bring her car around, she shifted anxiously on her feet while casting quick glances back toward the mansion's doors to make sure she hadn't been followed.

Just as her vehicle came around the curved driveway, she heard a very distinctive male voice from behind her yell out, "Hey! *Wait!*"

Oh, shit. She didn't have to look over her shoulder to know it was him. The urgency and confusion in his deep voice spoke for itself. She willed the kid in her car to *hurry up*, and as soon as he brought the vehicle to a stop and exited, Raina quickly got behind the wheel before she changed her mind and did exactly as the man ordered and *waited for him*.

"Goddamn it, *stop!*"

He reached her car just as she shut and locked the door. Because she couldn't bring herself to look at him, out of the corner of her eye she saw him stop right by the driver's door.

"I don't even know your name!" he said, sounding both bewildered and extremely pissed off that she'd stood him up without an explanation.

No names exchanged, and she planned to keep things that way. She'd never see him again, so what did it matter? Self-preservation edged out the regret tightening in her chest, and she pressed her foot on the gas pedal and drove away, resisting the temptation to look in her rear-view mirror to drink him in one last time.

She felt like Cinderella escaping her

prince before the clock struck twelve and she turned into a pumpkin. But instead of leaving behind a glass slipper, she realized he still had her *panties* tucked away in his pocket.

Well, at least she'd left him with a sexy souvenir of their one night together.

Find out what happens between Raina and her sexy, gorgeous stranger in the full-length novel PLAYING WITH TEMPTATION.

If you would like to know when my newest book will be released, please sign up for my newsletter here:
www.erikawilde.com/social-newsletter-sign-up

Other Books in
The Marriage Diaries Series
THE MARRIAGE DIARIES
THE INVITATION
THE CAPTURE

To learn more about Erika Wilde and

her upcoming releases, you can visit her at the following places on the web:

Website: www.erikawilde.com

Facebook: facebook.com/erikawildeauthorfanpage

Goodreads: goodreads.com/erikawildeauthor

Made in the USA
Middletown, DE
07 March 2024